C000149635

Borrowing Second Chances

Borrowing Amor, Volume 6

Kat Bellemore

Published by Kat Bellemore, 2019.

Chapter One

Debbie sauntered out of Town Hall feeling rejuvenated. She often heard others complaining about the weekly town council meetings, but she loved them. This fact had caught her by surprise after she had been elected to the council, considering she wasn't usually inclined to get involved in politics. As long as she had her beauty salon, she was happy.

But hearing the concerns of her friends and neighbors, and having the power to do something about it—that was refreshing. And there was certainly an abundance of concerns as the town saw more traffic and more high-end shops and restaurants moving in because of the space tourism industry that had set up less than an hour away.

"Debbie, hold up," someone called from behind her.

Debbie paused and looked back. Rebecca, the owner of the local bakery, was walking quickly toward her. Debbie whipped back around, but Rebecca already had a hand on Debbie's arm before she could escape.

"I noticed you were unusually quiet when I brought up the concern about another bakery opening within the next few months," Rebecca said.

Debbie turned back toward the baker with a forced smile. "I didn't have anything to add to the matter. I think the other council members covered it pretty well."

Rebecca balked. "The town doesn't need two bakeries."

"You're right," Debbie said. But before Rebecca's satisfied smile could completely settle in place, Debbie added, "The town needs three bakeries. Unfortunately, two is all we'll have for right now."

Rebecca's lips pulled downward and she sputtered, "Three? Are you trying to put me out of business?"

"Not at all. If I need a beautiful cake, I know where to go. But you don't bake breads, or bagels, or anything someone might want to grab on the go. We all have our specialties, and there is room for all of them in Amor."

"I thought you were elected to represent the needs of small business owners," Rebecca said.

"I was, and I am." Debbie now felt like her personal integrity was being attacked. She pulled her arm from Rebecca's grasp and tried to keep her patience. "Growth and change isn't easy, but I think we've all seen over the past year that it is necessary."

"Says the woman whose hair doesn't stay the same color for more than a month at a time." Rebecca eyed Debbie's blond hair. "I liked it better pink." Rebecca then spun on her heel and stalked away.

A long sigh released from between Debbie's lips, making a whistling sound. Okay, normally, she felt rejuvenated after those meetings. And then there were the times when they made her want to climb back into bed with a bowl of ice cream.

"You handled that well."

Debbie turned. Zoe stood there in her pantsuit, looking all official to perform her new mayoral duties. She had been the previous mayor's assistant for years and had been the one to help begin the transition from small town to tourist town, so it had been natural for her to take the mayor's place. It was a good look on her.

"She doesn't think I'm protecting her rights as a business owner," Debbie said. She knew she couldn't please everyone, but Rebecca's remarks had bothered Debbie just the same.

Zoe smiled. "She'll come around. Rebecca will always be the last to change her ways, but she can't deny how all the tourist money is improving our town."

Debbie nodded but didn't respond right away. Things were certainly busier, and a lot of improvements had been made, including the town finally getting an urgent care for those times when the doctor's office was closed. But Amor had managed to retain its small-town charm through it all, and Debbie attributed that to Zoe and Sam, the previous mayor.

"Well, everyone else seems to be happy with their booming businesses," Debbie said, forcing her thoughts away from Rebecca.

"Which brings me to a topic I was hoping to talk with you about." Zoe's formal tone conveyed that she was now speaking as Mayor McAllister, and it piqued Debbie's curiosity. "Let's walk back to your salon."

"What can I help you with? Do you need a perm?" Debbie teased.

Zoe smiled but shook her head. She remained silent as they walked down the sidewalk toward the newly renovated downtown, where one was just as likely to meet a celebrity preparing for their space flight as they were to meet a local resident of Amor. It wasn't until they were halfway to the salon that Zoe spoke.

"You're very good with people."

Debbie threw a curious glance toward the mayor. That was an interesting way to start a conversation. "Thank you," she said slowly.

"We are growing very quickly, not with permanent residents, but with businesses and tourists," Zoe continued. "Too quickly. We can't keep up. We can't supply the number of employees we need. Even at Town Hall, we have people working long hours to make up the difference."

Debbie had noticed, but she didn't know what this had to do with her.

"I'm sending out a recruiter to help draw people in." Then, with a side glance at Debbie, Zoe said, "and I'd like you to go along."

Debbie choked on her own spit. "Huh?" was all she managed to say in return.

Zoe smiled, though she was no longer looking at Debbie. "You would help recruit college students for the seasonal businesses, and recent graduates for the more permanent positions. We need people to move to Amor to manage the infrastructure we're building."

"Won't people naturally move to where there is opportunity?" Debbie asked, finally finding her voice.

"Eventually," Zoe said with a nod. "But we can't wait for nature to take its course. We need people now."

"But why me?"

"Like I said, you're good with people, and you represent the local businesses of Amor. You have a couple of employees at the salon now, right? Could they spare you for a week?"

Debbie's thoughts whirled. "Yes, I'm sure they'd be fine, as long as it's not longer than that. How many of us would be traveling around and recruiting?"

"Three. And you'll be paid for your time, of course."

Earning money while her salon continued to make money for her back home was tempting. Heaven knew she needed it. The expansion of her salon had cost more than Debbie had expected, and her bank account was still feeling it.

"All right. When do I leave?"

"Is this weekend too soon?"

"As in...three days from now?"

Zoe gave Debbie a side glance. "That won't be a problem, will it? I just need to finalize a few things with a couple of universities before you leave, and that will give you time to go over the technical details with our recruiter. He's very good at what he does and will make sure everything runs smoothly."

Debbie had been about to say that would be fine, but at Zoe's words, her jaw tightened.

"The recruiter is a 'he?'" Debbie had assumed she'd be traveling with the mayor's assistant, Sarah. It was the type of thing Zoe would have done when she was a mayoral assistant.

"You'll have separate hotel rooms, if that's what you're worried about," Zoe said quickly, though she seemed to be purposely avoiding Debbie's gaze now.

Debbie squinted in suspicion, then stepped in front of the mayor, facing her. "Who is he?"

Zoe's expression held so much guilt that Debbie suspected she hadn't been chosen for this recruiting trip for only her people skills.

"You're busy. I shouldn't keep you," Zoe said, her gaze flitting across the street.

"I'm not busy," Debbie said, not letting the mayor sidestep her question.

"You might not be busy now, but you will be in about ten seconds." Zoe nodded to where Debbie's salon sat across the street.

When Debbie turned, she saw that one of the front windows was broken and her stylists were frantically trying to clean up the glass. One of them looked up and saw Debbie. As their gazes met, Debbie saw the stylist's complexion pale.

"Looks like I know how I'll be using that extra money that you'll be paying me," Debbie said with a long sigh.

"Don't you have insurance?"

"Yeah, and a crazy high deductible."

Zoe grimaced. "I'm sorry. That's rotten luck. And your new salon only opened a couple of months ago. Come by my office tomorrow afternoon and we'll talk more. Maybe around four-thirty? I promise it won't take long." She walked quickly in the opposite direction, not giving Debbie the chance to answer.

Debbie knew that the mayor was known for her unconventional antics, and as she watched Zoe's retreating back, she couldn't shake the feeling that this was one of them. Zoe had looked too guilty for it to not be.

As Debbie hurried across the street to find out how the window on her salon had broken, she had to shove her suspicions aside. She'd find out soon enough.

Chapter Two

B ob rubbed his temples, fighting a looming headache. He knew it was going to rear its head as soon as he stopped working. He pressed 'submit' on the upcoming payroll, then glanced at the clock. Four-fifteen. He was at a good stopping point and could call it a day. That was what a normal person would do. But 'normal' didn't describe Bob. And the clock didn't say five o'clock, which meant he had to keep going for another forty-five minutes. What could he do that was productive but wouldn't suck up more time than that?

He had just decided to go over the slides he'd made for the new employee orientation that he'd be delivering the next morning, when Mayor McAllister poked her head in.

"Oh good, you're still here," she said with an over-the-top smile. The new mayor did that a lot.

He tried to return the smile, but his headache made the attempt feel more like a grimace. "Of course. It's not five yet," he said, nodding toward the clock.

"Perfectly true." She paused, then asked, "Can I speak with you in my office? It won't take more than a few minutes."

Bob stared. The mayor never called him into her office. "You can't tell me here?"

Mayor McAllister seemed like she was going to agree with his request, but when an employee from another department entered the office to use the laminating machine, she said, "I'd rather talk in private, if you don't mind."

Bob looked around the HR office. He only had one Human Resources employee, and he happened to be out sick. That would mean closing the office early. It wasn't just this that bothered him, though. Bob didn't like impromptu meetings. He wanted to know what it was about—to be able to plan ahead. Had he done something wrong that he didn't know about?

It was at that moment that Bob's headache decided to settle in right behind his eyes, and he tried to keep his annoyance at bay. He'd rather wait to speak with the mayor until the next day when he was feeling better, but whatever she had to say seemed important, and his curiosity was just as insistent as his headache.

"Does meeting in my office make you uncomfortable?" Mayor McAllister asked, her brows scrunched in concern. "We can leave my door open, if you'd prefer."

Bob realized he'd been staring into space, rubbing his forehead as he willed his headache to simmer down. She probably thought he was uncomfortable about a private meeting in her office because she was the first female mayor that Amor had ever had.

"No, that won't be necessary," Bob said. He waited until the employee using the laminating machine was finished, then stepped out of the office and locked the door behind him. He didn't move right away. What if there was an employee emergency? Would they know where to find him?

"You all right?" Mayor McAllister asked.

"Yes, of course." Bob straightened his shoulders and walked with long strides toward the mayor's office.

Mayor McAllister entered after him and sat down at a large desk. She motioned toward one of the chairs across from her. "Have a seat."

Bob nodded, then lowered himself slowly until he sat on the seat. It had a worn feeling to it, and he made a mental note that he should try to sit on the one on the left next time.

"As you know, we've been hiring in many of our divisions lately," the mayor started. "You have the orientation prepared for tomorrow morning?"

The mayor didn't need to ask; she knew it would already be done. Maybe she thought that asking about it was the polite thing to do. But Bob still felt insulted at the insinuation that he might not already have prepared his presentation. He decided to stay quiet and he gave a single nod.

"Good," she said. She interlaced her fingers and eyed Bob with a thoughtful look. Seconds ticked by, and he wondered if that was all she had wanted to ask him. Before he could ask if there was anything else, Mayor McAllister straightened and said, "I have a special assignment for you."

Bob's anxiety returned full throttle. Whenever someone used the word *special*, it was code for, *You aren't going to like this, so I'm going to try to make it seem like a good thing.* He remained silent, his thoughts racing with worst-case scenarios. The most unsettling was the possibility that she'd transfer him to the tourism department. Like Amor didn't already have too many tourists.

"I've never asked you to travel," the mayor said. "Up until now, your position hasn't required it." She stopped and seemed like she was gearing up for whatever would come next. "I need you to visit a few career fairs over the next week on a recruiting assignment."

That got Bob's attention, but there was no way he could have heard the mayor correctly. No one would purposely send him on a recruiting assignment. He'd be their last choice.

"I don't understand," he said.

"I need you to travel to colleges and universities around the state. We have a desperate need for employees as the tourism industry has expanded more rapidly than we could have predicted."

"I'm not the man for that kind of assignment," Bob said, still confused on what the mayor was asking him to do, or at least *why* she was asking him to do it. "You have plenty of employees who would be way better at that than I would."

"I made my choice," she said. "It's you."

Bob stared. She was serious? "Why? You know I'm terrible with people. If I go, no one is going to want to visit Amor, let alone come and work here."

"That is your opinion, and I don't agree," the mayor said. "But in simpler terms, as the manager of Human Resources, it's in your job description. You are in charge of recruiting."

Bob frowned. He had never paid attention to that part of the description because he'd never thought he'd ever have to do it. But he couldn't argue with the logic of having to do something because it was his job. Bob slid back down into his chair. "When do I leave?"

The mayor seemed surprised, like maybe she'd expected more of a fight out of him, but she quickly regained her composure. "You will leave this weekend. Your first career fair is on Monday."

Bob tried to hold back a grimace. "Okay." He glanced at his watch. Four-thirty. "Anything else?"

"There is one more thing," the mayor said. Before she could tell him what that thing was, she was interrupted by the office door opening.

"Would you look at that, I'm right on time," a woman's voice said.

Bob expected the mayor to tell the woman that she was interrupting a private conversation, but when the mayor didn't, but instead looked like she'd been expecting the woman, he turned in his seat to see who it was.

She stood in the doorway to the office, her long blond hair hanging over one shoulder. Her hair was smooth—the type that made you want to run your fingers through it. But it was when his gaze moved to her face that his heart stuttered.

Debbie.

He hadn't seen her much since she'd moved her salon over to the touristy side of town. Her hair was longer, and no longer purple like the last time she'd asked him to notarize some paperwork. But her eyes were still the same bright blue.

She noticed him at the same time and her mouth dropped open, but just a little. Enough to send Bob's pulse racing.

"I-I'm sorry," she stuttered. "I didn't realize you were in a meeting." She spoke as if to the mayor, but her gaze never left Bob.

In that moment, it was as if they had never broken up. She still undid every nerve and left him speechless. He never could think rationally around Debbie. After they had split up a couple of years before, it had taken months for Bob to be able to function normally—or at least what was normal for him. He was the town's only notary, so Debbie had no choice but to come see him on occasion. But she never allowed herself to look him in the eyes as she was doing at the moment.

That wasn't entirely true. There had been that one time a little over a year ago when she was selling her old salon to a real estate developer and Bob had tried to stop her from signing the paperwork. That hadn't been his finest moment, and Debbie had seemed to agree when she'd stormed out.

What was she doing here? Her proximity made him want to relive their first kiss and remind her of what they'd had—what they had given up. The memory of the way she'd sat on his lap while he was in her styling chair, her breath tickling his ear, made blood rush to his cheeks. Just the thought of her lips on his made his skin clammy, and he had the urge to pull her close right then and there.

But then the mayor spoke, and reality came crashing in. Debbie had broken up with him, and she was happier now. She was too spontaneous and full of life to be happy with someone like Bob.

"I actually wanted both of you here," Mayor McAllister was telling Debbie. "I know this whole thing is short notice, but the colleges and universities we contacted took their time in getting back to us."

"Why do we both need to be here?" Debbie asked slowly.

"Because you'll be working together on this project."

Bob's gaze snapped back to the mayor. "What?"

"You'll be traveling together. As a team."

Debbie's gaze flickered to Bob, then back to the mayor. Her features were contorted in panic, and it made Bob bristle. Was spending time with him, even in a professional capacity, so awful to evoke that kind of reaction?

"When you said I'd be working with a recruiter, you purposely chose not to tell me who it would be," Debbie said to the mayor, her voice low. "You know about our past."

"Yes, I do," Mayor McAllister said, still bright and chipper, as if they were talking about the unusual amount of rain they'd had that summer. "But I also know that you are both the best people for the job. Bob will make sure everything runs smoothly, and you'll be the one who can talk to people about the impact that tourism has had on local businesses, and the town in general."

Bob hated to admit it, but it made sense. Debbie could make someone want to live in a van by a river, never mind a thriving tourism town.

"And we'll be driving separately?" she asked, her tone hopeful.

"Of course not," the mayor said. "That would be a waste of gas as well as a safety issue. I'd never send anyone alone, driving all over the desert." Her eyes sparkled, like she was enjoying herself.

If Bob didn't know any better, he'd say she'd purposely picked the two of them *because* of their past. Scratch that. That seemed exactly the kind of thing the new mayor would do. Just because she had a different title didn't mean she'd changed at all. For better or worse, she had been born a matchmaker.

His gaze flickered toward Debbie, who he was surprised to see had now narrowed her eyes and was glaring at the mayor.

"Really, Zoe?" Debbie asked. "I agreed to do this for you, not because I had to, but because you needed me."

"And you need the money for your salon, right?" Mayor McAllister asked. "I need someone who is good with people. Is it my fault that I also need someone who is good with the logistics, and that person happens to be your ex-boyfriend?"

The conversation was taking a turn that made Bob both uncomfortable and hurt. He didn't want to see how badly Debbie wanted to get away from him, or how she would turn down money just to not have to sit in the same car as him.

He stood and backed toward the door, but someone else was just stepping in, blocking his path of escape.

Mayor McAllister looked at whoever had just entered the room, and relief smoothed out the mayor's features. "Sandy, I'm glad you were able to make it."

Bob turned and saw Sandy, the baker's daughter. She tucked a strand of her short brown hair behind one ear. "I'm sorry I'm late," she said. "Mother doesn't approve of this at all, and it took some convincing for her to allow me to come."

Mayor McAllister raised an eyebrow. "Oh? I thought she had agreed that this would be a positive thing for you."

"Cold feet, I guess."

The mayor turned her attention to Bob and Debbie. "You both know Sandy, don't you?"

Bob and Debbie both nodded, but Bob couldn't have spoken if he'd wanted to. His surprise at seeing Sandy in the mayor's office equaled the surprise he'd felt when he had seen Debbie. Sandy rarely went out, and when she did, she was usually helping her mother at the bakery. Rebecca kept a pretty short leash on her daughter, despite the fact that Sandy was an adult, and had been for quite some time. Sandy had to be around twenty-five or twenty-six, but was as dependent on her mother as a young child.

"Sandy will be your other travel companion," Mayor McAllister said.

When the mayor had first told Bob that he'd be leaving on a recruiting trip, he'd thought she was being funny. When he'd said that Debbie would be joining him, he'd thought she was being cruel. But adding Sandy to the mix? This was beyond anything Bob could define.

Mayor McAllister was unique, but she was good at what she did, which was why the town had elected her in the first place. But why would she send Sandy? The woman hadn't left Amor in at least a decade, and she hadn't made a decision for herself in just as long. She was certainly no better at talking with people than he was.

Bob was trying to figure out how to tactfully ask about the mayor's unusual choice when Sandy answered the question herself.

"I know what you're thinking, Mr. Larcher." She gave him a smile that told him she wasn't offended. "I promise I won't hold you back. Think of me as your ball boy...or woman, in this case." Her eyes brightened. "I like the sound of that. Ball woman," she said again, as if testing the sound on her tongue. "Whatever you need, just ask and I'll get it for you. No job is too small. No job is too...well, there may be some jobs that are too big, just as a forewarning. My therapist has said I've made a lot of progress over the last year, but I'm still working on a few things."

"Uh-huh," Bob said. He tried to smile, but his headache, which had been replaced by the shock of the situation he had found himself in, had returned full force. "We can go over the details later, but I do have a couple of things I'd like to get done before I head home for the night," he said, once again backing toward the open doorway.

"Before you go, I just wanted to let you know that I'll have the itinerary on your desk in the morning," Mayor McAllister said. "Let me know if you have any questions about it." She didn't seem as confident as she had before, almost like she was second-guessing her decision to throw the three of them together for a whole week. Good. Maybe she'd call the whole thing off.

He gave a quick nod, then, without glancing back, he hurried back down the hall to the HR office. He stood outside the locked door, trying to process everything that had just happened.

Seven days. With Debbie.

Bob no longer felt the need to stay until five o'clock, and quickly left the building.

He didn't want to risk the possibility of running into her again on his way out.

And it was obvious that she would rather not see him either.

Chapter Three

Debbie lay in bed, staring at the ceiling. She flopped over and looked at her phone for the fiftieth time. Six o'clock. Bob wouldn't be by to pick her up until eight, but she might as well get up. It wasn't like she was going to get any sleep. She made herself a cup of coffee, then busied herself with double-checking her suitcase.

Debbie checked her phone again. Six-thirty. Ugh. She still had an hour and a half to kill.

After making scrambled eggs and toast, she realized she still wore her rocket ship pajamas. She wanted to be comfortable for the road trip, but traveling with other people was different than traveling by herself. And traveling with Bob was a different thing entirely.

It wasn't like she cared what the man thought of her. Obviously. And yet, she found herself trying out several pairs of pants, all of which would have been just fine, and not being able to decide on any of them.

Maybe a nice pair of yoga pants. They were certainly comfortable, and they accented her figure in a way that boosted her confidence, which she could certainly use at the moment.

Debbie tried on a black pair and was pleased to see they looked even better on her than they had the last time she had checked. It turned out that her exercise classes were actually working.

Her smile morphed into horror. What was she thinking? She couldn't wear those around Bob. Nothing that accented her curves the way those pants did could be worn around him. She tore them off, then looked for the baggiest, frumpiest pair of jeans in her closet. Sure, they wouldn't be as comfortable, but she needed to make sure she drew a line concerning proper ex-girlfriend etiquette for a business trip.

Of course, if she wore something that showed off her figure, she'd also be showing Bob what he was missing out on. She eyed the yoga pants on the floor and picked them back up.

Debbie fingered the fabric for a moment before giving a quick shake of her head. "No," she yelled, throwing them across the room, as if they were poisonous. "You evil temptress yoga pants. He broke my heart. He doesn't deserve you."

By the time she had settled on a pair of baggy capris, a loose top, and her hair pulled back into a ponytail, the time had been spent, and there was a knock at the door.

Debbie stared, knowing she needed to open it, but not wanting to.

Bob was on the other side. The man she'd tried to avoid for the past two years, which had been difficult, given the small town they lived in. Occasionally she had caught his gaze in passing and a flicker of hope had returned, but then he'd quickly look away, and the flame extinguished before it could fully ignite.

And now she had to spend the next week with him.

Debbie was tempted to call Zoe and tell her the deal was off. But Debbie needed the money. She had a business she was trying to grow, and the broken window was just another thing on the long list of items she needed.

Another knock sounded on the door, this one louder than the previous one.

With a long exhale, Debbie reached for the doorknob. She figured it was like removing a Band-Aid. The longer it took, the more painful. She counted to three, then flung the door open.

Bob stood on her porch, and yet, it wasn't him. He looked incredible in a loose T-shirt and blue jeans. And was that stubble on his chin?

What was happening?

Bob didn't do casual, and he certainly didn't skip his morning shave.

He shifted under her gaze and looked at his watch. "Am I early?" he asked, his eyebrows scrunched together, as if concerned that he had been anything but punctual.

Debbie realized she was gaping, and she snapped her mouth shut. "No, sorry. I'll grab my suitcase."

She hurried inside and had to take a few calming breaths. So what if Bob looked amazing? He was still the man who had been too embarrassed by her to tell anyone they were dating.

With her head held high, Debbie grabbed the handle of her suitcase and walked resolutely out the door. She would no longer allow that man to have power over her.

Her determination collapsed when Bob reached to take the luggage from her.

"I can take that for you," he said.

He was being a perfect gentleman, which was not at all what Debbie had been expecting. Why couldn't he be as awkward as she felt? It was the least he could do after being placed in this situation. Debbie was pretty sure Zoe had known exactly what she was doing when she asked the two of them to go on this trip together. But whatever good intentions the mayor had, it wasn't going to work. Debbie was not getting back together with her ex-boyfriend.

Bob took the handle from Debbie when she failed to respond, and she watched him haul the suitcase over to his car.

"Why don't you make sure everything is turned off before we head out?" he called over.

Oh, so that was why he had taken the suitcase from her. Mr. Responsible wanted to make sure that Debbie was following the safety procedures of leaving on an extended trip. Of course. He probably even had a checklist that he expected her to follow.

"I was just about to take care of that," Debbie said, then walked back into the house. She lazily glanced into the living room, then her bedroom, making sure she hadn't forgotten anything. She caught a glimpse of her phone charger over by her nightstand and grabbed it. All the lights were off in the bedrooms, but when she reached the kitchen, she realized she'd left on the burner that had been cooking her eggs. Luckily the frying pan was no longer on the stove, but that could have been bad. She quickly turned it off, then made sure nothing else was on that shouldn't be.

Debbie wasn't going to give Bob credit for the narrow miss, though. She would have double-checked, even without his reminder. Maybe.

When she stepped back out onto the front porch and shut the door, he looked up from where he stood by the car. He now had sunglasses on, and Debbie's heart pounded against her ribcage. Sunglasses were another first, and they were working for him in all the right ways. She began wondering if Bob was even the same man she'd dated.

"Did you make sure all the doors and windows are locked?" he asked.

Yup, he was the same man.

"Yes, but I can check again, if it would make you feel better," she said, her heartbeat slowing to a reasonable tempo.

"If you don't mind, it would."

Debbie spun back toward the house and moved to unlock the front door. Except, it turned out no key was needed. It wasn't locked.

Oops.

And apparently neither were three windows and the back door. Debbie didn't want to think that Bob had been right about that too. But seriously, who worried about those types of things in Amor? It was the safest place on the planet. Though Debbie did know of several people who had taken to locking up with the influx of tourists in the past year.

Once she had triple-checked that everything was off, things were locked, and the garbage had been taken out, they were finally ready to leave.

Debbie opened the passenger door and noticed Sandy watching them quietly from the back seat. Debbie had momentarily forgotten there was someone besides Bob coming on this trip. That would help relieve any tension on the drive.

"Hi, Sandy," Debbie said, not moving to get into the car. "Did you want to sit up front?" She crossed her fingers behind her back.

Please say yes. Please say yes.

"No, it's okay. I tried it out on our way here and I felt like the road was rushing at me," Sandy said in a chipper voice.

"Oh...all right." Debbie slid into her seat with a sense of dread. This was going to be a long week.

The key was already in the ignition, but Bob didn't move to turn the car on. "Are you okay if I drive the whole way? It's only about six hours to the first city we'll be staying in, and I feel more comfortable behind the wheel."

"Six?" Debbie asked, pulling out her phone. That couldn't be right. "I thought it was only four hours."

"I analyzed the time of day and the various routes, and because of its propensity for car accidents and construction, the four-hour route often takes much longer."

Debbie stared. When they had dated, she had loved when Bob spoke like that—it was actually what had begun many of their kissing sessions. It was because of him that she'd realized that she was incredibly attracted to intelligent men. "That sounds fine. I know you wouldn't steer us wrong," she said, her voice a little hoarse. But then she thought about what she'd just said and couldn't trap the giggle that bubbled up. "Steer us wrong...and you're driving...get it? I'm funny without even trying."

Laughter erupted from the back seat. "That was a good one," Sandy choked out. She was laughing so hard that tears were running down her face.

Okay, it hadn't been *that* funny.

Bob's lip turned up like he might smile, but then settled back down.

So, that was how this trip was going to be.

Debbie looked out the window as he started the car and turned on the GPS. This was so weird. She was driving with Bob. Her Bob. Or the Bob who had once been hers. The last time they had spoken, she had been so furious with him that she had stormed out of Town Hall. It wasn't like they had been on speaking terms before that, but now? They were most definitely not on speaking terms. But what were they supposed to do, be in the same enclosed space and not talk for six days?

Maybe. Because she had nothing to say to this man. Well, nothing that would make a difference. If she told him what she thought of him, right at that moment, it wouldn't be pretty, and the rest of their time together would be worse than it already was.

But as she caught his reflection in the window, her breathing turned shallow. She tried to shake off the feelings that his presence still brought to the surface. Debbie couldn't still be in love with Bob. She wouldn't allow it. He had burned that bridge a long time ago.

"I brought snacks," he said, breaking into Debbie's thoughts. He pointed over his shoulder to the back seat. "I know you love potato chips, but you could never decide which flavor was your favorite, so I just bought one of everything."

Debbie glanced back, and sure enough, scattered around Sandy were about ten bags of potato chips, along with grapefruit juice and a bag of chocolates. All her favorites. She quickly turned back to the window, not wanting Bob to see the reaction he had elicited.

He had remembered. This was why she had loved him. Because he had been one of the kindest people she had ever met. Other people didn't understand him, and truthfully, she didn't always understand him either. But he was real. And their relationship had gone deeper than the physical side of things, though he certainly wasn't lacking in that department. He had always treated her like she was the most amazing person in the world—when they were alone.

When they were in public, that was a different story. In those situations, they were acquaintances, at best—two people who knew of each other, and happened to be in the same place at the same time.

Oh boy. She was in trouble. Because Bob was acting like he had when they were dating.

Debbie had to make sure they weren't alone. Ever.

No matter how much she hated to admit it, she realized she still couldn't trust herself around him, and if he was buying all her favorite foods, she didn't trust him either.

Chapter Four

B ob glanced across to where Debbie dozed in the passenger
seat, and he had to force his gaze back to the road. She had
barely looked at him since he'd pointed out the snacks he had
bought for the road trip. Maybe he had overstepped a boundary.

He hadn't slept at all the night he had discovered that he'd
be on this road trip with Debbie, his brain refusing to shut off.
He couldn't stop thinking about her reaction to the news, and
he wondered how he was expected to act around her. They were
technically colleagues for the time being, and he would treat her as
such if that was what she wanted. But he also wanted to make her
as comfortable as possible with the situation. She obviously wasn't
happy about it, and he had thought that if he dressed more casually
and brought her favorite snacks, it would help.

Apparently not.

The woman hadn't so much as glanced his way in two hours.
Granted, she had been sleeping for half of it, but still.

After driving in the desert with no signs of civilization for what
seemed like forever, Bob noticed a sign indicating that a gas station
was off the next exit. They were well on their way to the first city on
their list, but the gas gauge was already showing that the tank was
half empty, and he liked to play it safe. Who knew when they'd hit
the next station? He eased the car off the freeway and onto the exit
ramp.

Once the tank was full, Bob moved the car to a parking spot. He turned in his seat and saw that Sandy was wide awake.

"I'm going to step in to use the restroom," he told her.

"Oh, I need it too," she said, practically leaping from the car. Sandy disappeared into the gas station, and Bob's gaze returned to Debbie.

He really needed to use the bathroom but wasn't sure if he should leave her. He knew it wasn't like he was leaving a child, but still, she would be completely unaware of her surroundings as she slept. What if something happened while he was inside?

An internal debate raged until his bladder ultimately decided the verdict.

Careful to lock all the doors as well as scan the parking lot for anyone who seemed sketchy, Bob hurried inside.

It took longer than he had anticipated, due to the bathroom having only one stall, and a small boy taking five times as long as Bob thought necessary. But as soon as he walked outside and saw his car, something seemed off.

Upon closer inspection, he realized that the passenger door was cracked open slightly, and with a quick glance, he saw that Debbie was no longer in the seat. His stomach dropped as he spun around, scanning the parking lot. Anyone who had been there had left. His was the only car.

Sandy wasn't back yet, and he hurried back inside.

"Have you seen Debbie?" he asked Sandy when she walked out of the bathroom.

"Nope. There's only one stall in there, and I was in it," Sandy said.

Bob whipped his phone out, not sure who he could call. Maybe the police? He punched 9-1-1 into the phone, but the call wouldn't go through. He had no service at the remote gas station.

Panic settled in.

Bob sprinted to the counter, where a young man sat, looking bored. "I need help. She's gone. I think someone took her. You have to call the police." His breath came out in gasps, and it felt like the room was closing in around him.

The attendant sat up, suddenly alert. "Of course. Can you tell me her name and how old she is?"

"Debra Allred," Bob said. "I think she's thirty, could be a couple years older, though. I don't remember exactly."

The attendant paused, his pen hanging between his fingers.

"Well, why aren't you writing it down?" Bob demanded.

"So...she's not a child," the attendant said slowly.

"What does that matter? She was asleep in the car, and now she's gone. It's not that complicated to understand."

The attendant rubbed his chin for a moment, then said, "Are you sure she didn't leave of her own accord?"

Bob released a sigh of exasperation. The longer this conversation continued, the further away Debbie would be. "Are you going to help me or not?"

Something in the distance seemed to have caught the attendant's eye because his gaze drifted, like he was bored of the conversation. "Let me ask you one more question," he said. "Is the woman you lost pretty, with long blond hair?"

"I didn't lose her, she was taken," Bob said, his voice unnaturally shrill. "And yes, she's beautiful. So what?"

"Is she wearing a yellow shirt with tan pants?"

"I think they are more like capris, but—" Bob's voice broke off. "You remember seeing her?" he asked, hope breaking through.

"Yeah, I remember seeing her," the attendant said. "She's waiting in line behind you, apparently wanting to buy a sandwich."

Bob spun around. Debbie stood there, confusion etched in her features.

"You're okay," he breathed out, then wrapped her in a hug. She stiffened under his arms, and he let go. "Sorry," he muttered. He was just so relieved to see her, and all in one piece. But that relief quickly transformed into frustration. "Where were you? I almost called the police."

"You sound like my father when I would stay out too late," Debbie said with a bemused smile. "Except, he never threatened to call the police over a five-minute bathroom break."

"Bathroom break?" Bob asked, staring.

"Yeah. I woke up in the car and when I realized where we were, I came in to use the restroom."

"But Sandy said she didn't see you in there."

"They have another one out back that they said I could use," she said.

Bob threw an irritated look at the attendant. He hadn't thought to tell Bob that tiny detail? "But your car door wasn't shut all the way," he said, turning back to Debbie.

"I'm sorry, I don't know anything about that." She laid some money on the counter. "But I didn't mean to worry you. Sorry." She looked into his eyes, and hers held raw honesty. She really did feel bad that she'd worried him.

"I suppose I may have overreacted," Bob admitted, following her back out to the car. It hadn't felt like it at the time, though. Why did he suddenly feel like it was his job to protect her? She was perfectly capable of taking care of herself. He knew that she carried pepper spray and had taken enough self-defense classes that he didn't ever want to be on the receiving end of one of her roundhouse kicks. And yet the feeling lingered.

Debbie walked to the passenger side and examined the door that was still ajar. "There's the culprit," she said, pulling on the seatbelt. "It blocked the door from shutting all the way."

"Don't you double-check before leaving the car?"

"Another lecture?" she asked, rolling her eyes, though she wore a small smile.

They slid into their seats, but before Bob was able to start the car, Debbie placed a hand on his arm and looked him in the eyes.

"Thank you," she said.

Bob swallowed hard. The warmth of her hand sent electric shocks through his nerves, and he was having trouble forming thoughts.

"For what?" he finally managed to say.

"For caring. I know that I worried you, but thank you for keeping me safe."

Bob hadn't thought that Debbie would ever thank him again for anything, but now that she had, he realized he didn't deserve it. "I should have trusted that you'd be fine sitting in a car for ten minutes," he said, shaking his head. "What you deserve is an apology. I almost had the cops out here."

Debbie's eyes crinkled at the corners, like she was trying not to laugh. "It would have added to the adventure."

Unwanted feelings bubbled up within Bob. The same ones that made him want to kiss Debbie so passionately that she'd forget her own name. She always lived life to the fullest, and she made Bob want to do the same. No one else had that effect on him. Those feelings had always scared him, but once Debbie had left and taken those feelings with her, his life had felt empty. Now, he was just getting a taste of what he'd lost, and it was already turning him inside-out.

But Debbie wanted nothing to do with him. She'd made that clear in the mayor's office.

A rustling from the back seat reminded Bob that they weren't alone, and he started the ignition.

If today was only day one of their journey, how on earth was he going to make it to day six?

Chapter Five

The prospect of being in the car for six hours hadn't seemed terrible when they had first started out on the road, but the last hour felt twice as long as the previous four. And they still had an hour to go.

"I hope you were right about this route being the correct choice," Debbie said, trying to stretch her legs in front of her. She checked the back seat to make sure Sandy wasn't in the way before sliding her own seat all the way back. Sandy was sitting behind Bob, her face glued to the window, like she'd never seen the passing scenery. And then Debbie remembered that Sandy probably hadn't.

"I was," Bob said. "I checked when we stopped at the last rest area. There was a three-car pileup on the other route." He sounded very pleased with himself, but then sent a concerned look her way. "Do you need me to stop at the next exit?"

Debbie twisted her back until she felt a gratifying pop. "No, it's okay. Let's just push through. These jalapeno cheddar chips will help me survive the last hour." She stole a glance at him, conflicted on how she should feel about this road trip. On one hand, she had convinced herself that she'd hate every minute of it. Stuck in a car with the man who broke her heart wasn't exactly her idea of a good time. Debbie had expected that she'd spend the entire trip giving him the silent treatment, and only speaking to him when necessary.

But the way he had reacted at the gas station when he thought something had happened to her—it had ignited everything she'd promised herself she wouldn't feel. Bob still cared about her, she knew he did. She hadn't witnessed the entire encounter with the gas station attendant, but she had seen enough to know that he would have done anything to find her.

So, why had he tossed her aside two years earlier? If he would do anything to keep her safe, why had he trampled all over her heart?

Bob turned and caught her gaze, and Debbie's head whipped back toward the other direction.

"How is your first day of freedom?" she asked, turning to Sandy. Debbie needed a distraction from Bob and his stubble. Why had no other man looked as good without shaving as he did?

Sandy glanced back at Debbie, then resumed watching the desert. "Amazing," she said. "I can't believe how beautiful it is. Did you see those hills that looked like they were made of boulders? They almost looked like they were rock creatures and could spring to life at any moment."

Debbie knew the hills that Sandy was talking about. And they really were that cool. "Do you mind if I ask you a personal question?"

"Not at all," Sandy said.

"How long has it been since you've been outside of Amor?"

Sandy paused and counted on her fingers. "Around fifteen years, I guess."

"That's a long time."

There was a long stretch of silence, and Debbie wondered if she had said something she shouldn't have.

"That was when my dad died," Sandy finally said.

"I'm sorry," Debbie said, her voice soft.

Sandy gave a small shrug. "It was unavoidable, something that no one could have stopped or predicted."

"It still had to have been hard."

"Yeah." Sandy's gaze returned to the passing scenery. "Overnight I became anxious about everything. What if I made a wrong choice without knowing it, and the same thing happened to me? Or what if my actions accidentally hurt someone else?" She paused. "I used to not be able to talk about it, but seeing a therapist has really helped, and he thought I was ready for something that would challenge me."

"Which is why you're here," Debbie guessed.

"Yup. I'm here for therapy. Being able to be away from my mother and make my own decisions is the next big step I needed to take. Zoe was nice enough to suggest this trip, and with a little convincing, my mother agreed to it." Sandy paused. "Though, between you and me, I think she was more anxious about it than I was. I've actually felt ready for a while now, and just needed to muster up the courage to take the plunge."

Bob spoke up, surprising Debbie. His voice was thoughtful as he said, "I know what it's like to be anxious all the time. If you think I'm bad now, you should have seen me as a kid. If there's anything we can do to help you, just let us know."

Debbie noticed that he had used the word 'we', but it felt right, like she and Bob were a team on a quest to help Sandy find her happiness.

"Thanks," Sandy said. "Just being able to tell you the real reason I'm here has lifted a weight off my mind."

The three of them fell back into silence, but it was now a comfortable one.

"You can choose a radio station if you like," Bob finally said, throwing a quick glance Debbie's way.

It wasn't like Bob to give up control of his radio. "Are you sure?" she asked, reaching for the dial.

Bob tilted his head to the side, like he wasn't sure if it was a serious question. "Of course."

Rather than turn the radio on, she sat back in her seat. "Why are you being so nice?" She blurted it out and immediately wished she could shove the words back in. So much for only speaking when necessary.

Bob's hands tightened around the steering wheel, and he was quiet for a moment. "Have I ever treated you otherwise?" he finally asked.

Debbie thought about it. Nope. He had never said a harsh word to her, even when they broke up. He'd gone so far as to call to check up on her the next day. It hadn't been how he'd spoken to her two years ago that had solidified their break-up, though. It had been the feeling she'd had after he'd said what he had to say. He'd been so matter-of-fact when he had told her he needed time to sort everything out—indefinitely. They had already been sneaking around for four months, and he still didn't want to be seen in public with her. He hadn't needed to say the words for the meaning to shine through loud and clear.

"No, you haven't. Not in private, anyway."

He raised an eyebrow. "What's that supposed to mean?"

Debbie glanced back at Sandy and saw she had fallen asleep, her head resting against the window.

"It means that as soon as we leave this car, you are going to go back to pretending I don't exist," Debbie whispered.

Bob's mouth gaped open, like he was shocked to be hearing this. But how could he be surprised? This was beginning to be a repeat of the conversation they'd had in the back of her salon.

After he had kissed her so hard and passionately that she'd thought her heart was going to explode. But then he had refused to be seen leaving the salon with her afterward.

"Why would I do that?" he whispered back "I've never been able to pretend you don't exist. Believe me, I've tried for the last two years." He seemed flustered by his admission. With a quick shake of his head, he said, "Besides, we're colleagues for the duration of this assignment. We need to be able to work together."

"So, you'll be seen with me as long as people expect it of you," Debbie muttered. "I guess I should have asked the mayor to assign me as your girlfriend when we started dating. Maybe then you wouldn't have broken up with me."

"Me break up with you? You have an interesting way of distorting history," Bob said with a frown.

"It's obvious that you didn't want to be seen dating me because it broke one of your precious rules. That's the only reason you do anything. I'm still not clear if dating, in general, broke your rules, or if it was just dating a woman like me." Debbie folded her arms across her chest, breathing heavily.

This was why she should have stuck to her own rule that she'd made for herself. The one about not talking to Bob on this trip. She was like a box of TNT, ready to blow, and if the conversation lasted any longer, she was sure the result wouldn't be pretty.

"Dating you had nothing to do with my rules. Besides, you said that was one of the things you loved about me," Bob said, his voice now so quiet that Debbie almost hadn't heard him. "You liked how my ability to draw a line in the sand about what was right and wrong made you feel secure. You said it helped balance out your spontaneity."

Yes, she had said that.

"I was wrong," she said in an equally quiet voice. But it still rang through the car.

This time, Bob didn't respond, and they stayed quiet until they reached their hotel.

THE NEXT MORNING, DEBBIE worked her way through the hotel's complimentary breakfast. It was probably complimentary because there was nothing edible. Who wanted old oatmeal that had been sitting out all morning? She grabbed a piece of toast and rubbery eggs and found a seat at a table on the other side of the room. Even if her hunger forced her to eat the food, at least she wouldn't have to smell it at the same time.

"You should have gone for the cold cereal," someone said from the next table.

With a quick glance, Debbie located the speaker. It was a man about her age whose hair looked like it hadn't been combed that morning. It stood up all over his head, and yet he still managed to look comparable to Cary Grant. He was looking straight at her, so she supposed his words were meant for her.

"I've been trying to stay away from dairy," Debbie said, patting down her hair and hoping she looked as good as he did straight out of bed.

The man's smile transformed into a funny look, like he wasn't sure why she was telling him this bit of information.

Debbie herself was confused, until a pretty brunette walked up from behind Debbie and sat down with the man.

"I know, but I can't resist sausage," the woman said. "Even if it *is* wiggly."

Heat rushed into Debbie's cheeks and she spun back around. Of course Cary Grant would have an Audrey Hepburn lookalike. She frowned and stabbed at her eggs. That yellow square on her plate definitely had not come from nature. She stood and threw her plate in the trash, then grabbed a bowl. She'd stay away from dairy later. It couldn't be worse than her other options at this point.

When she turned back to find her table, a bowl of Frosted Flakes and a cup of orange juice in hand, she saw that her table had been taken, as had all the others. She spotted Bob sitting at a table with Sandy in the back corner and she steeled herself. It was just breakfast. He'd understand her needing to find somewhere to sit. And his table was on the opposite side of the room from Cary Grant, which was a plus.

"Good, you didn't get the eggs," Bob said as she slid into a chair at the table. "They were awful. If I end up sick later, you'll know why."

Debbie stared for a moment. He was acting so...normal. He treated her as if they were friends, or at least on speaking terms. It was as if their conversation the day before had never happened.

"I did, but I couldn't bring myself to eat them. Someone suggested cold cereal," she finally said.

Sandy held up her fork, where a circular piece of meat hung. At least, Debbie thought that was what it could be. Like the eggs, it wasn't completely clear.

"I totally agree," Sandy said. "But I could eat this sausage all day. Maybe it's the grease or the extra salt or something else that I don't want to know about. But it's Heaven."

"I thought you only eat chicken fried steak," Debbie said, shoveling in a spoonful of her cereal. Last she'd heard, Sandy could only order one thing at the diner she ate at several times a week.

"That was before the last challenge my therapist gave me. I was supposed to order something different each time I went to the diner." Sandy shuddered. "Those first few weeks were not pretty. For anyone." She straightened her shoulders and she had a look of pride. "But I can now order anything, even from places I've never been, and actually enjoy it."

"Sounds like your therapist is a miracle worker." Debbie tried to not let her gaze rove in Bob's direction.

Sandy dug around in her purse for a moment, then produced a business card. "Here. She's pretty booked up, but if you ever feel like you need someone, give her a call and mention my name. I'm sure she could fit you in."

"Thanks," Debbie said, fingering the card before slipping it into her pocket.

"Well, I'm done," Sandy said around one last bite of sausage. "See you back up at the room?" she asked Debbie.

"Yeah, then we can go over the plan for the day."

"Sounds good." Sandy dumped her trash, then disappeared among the rest of the breakfast goers.

She was hardly recognizable from the woman that Debbie had thought she'd known. Of course, Sandy was usually one of those people who lingered in the background and didn't attract attention. She had probably changed right before their eyes, and no one had even noticed.

Debbie ate another bite of cereal, but nearly choked when she realized that Bob was watching her.

His gaze dropped back to his own empty plate. "I'm sorry about yesterday," he said.

First, he had acted like their conversation hadn't happened, and now he was confronting it head-on. Didn't the man know that those types of things were supposed to be avoided? He wasn't supposed to talk to her at all, but just hope that the memory of their past would eventually lift and disappear, like an early morning fog.

But he looked back up at her, as if expecting her to respond.

This time it was Debbie's turn to drop her gaze. She shoved another spoonful of Frosted Flakes into her mouth to buy an extra minute. She finally had no choice but to swallow. "It seems we have a difference of opinion on what happened in my salon that evening. But none of that really matters now. We're here for a job, nothing more—nothing less. Zoe needs us to convince people that Amor is the place they want to work, and get them to move there."

Bob interlocked his fingers behind his head, and he leaned back in his chair. He was quiet for a moment, before saying, "I'll feel like I'm lying to everyone."

"But you love Amor."

"Yes, but I have to pretend I want them there. And I don't. I mean, I know the town is growing and money is pouring in faster than we know how to use it. We can't sustain this pace forever without more people to support the growth, but I miss the quieter days."

Debbie understood that sentiment; they had all experienced it at one time or another. But she couldn't deny loving how busy her salon was now and meeting new people from all around the world. She found it kind of exciting.

"Well, lucky for you, your job here is to make sure all the details are in place so that I can do the sweet talking," Debbie said.

Bob sat back up in his chair, and his arms dropped to his sides. "Let's get to it, then."

"Can I ask you a favor first?" she asked.

"Sure."

"Can we not talk about anything personal while we're here? Maybe we could add it to your list of rules."

"You want a rule stating that we won't talk about anything other than business," Bob said slowly.

Debbie nodded. She couldn't handle any more awkward arguments over something that still made her heart ache, even after all this time. Just eating at the same table was enough to nearly undo her. The man was as frustrating as he was good looking, but he had always kept things interesting, and he had a good heart. She had always delighted in the fact that she had something special with Bob that no one else had discovered yet. He was like her diamond in the rough.

"Fine, if that's what you want," he said, standing and gathering up his empty plate and cup.

It wasn't what she wanted, but it was what she needed.

Chapter Six

B ob stepped aside to avoid yet another college student on an electric scooter. Since when had those become a thing? He didn't understand it—why couldn't they just walk to class like he had when he had gone to school? Was exercise out of fashion, or was everyone in just too much of a rush to get where they were going? He thought of electric scooters inundating Amor and an involuntary shudder traveled down his spine.

He turned to Debbie to get her opinion about the scooters, but two things stopped him. First, he remembered the new rule about keeping their conversations to business-only topics. But it was the second thing that made not only him but also his breath come to a standstill.

It was the look on her face as her gaze moved across the college campus—her eyes so full of wonder and life that they were practically dancing. She seemed like she was trying to soak everything in, but she couldn't do it fast enough. She watched the people on scooters, then her attention shifted to students studying under a large tree. Her gaze lingered on a couple who were kissing on a bench, and it wasn't until she noticed Bob watching her that she looked down at the ground, pink rushing into her cheeks.

"I always wondered what it would be like to go to college," she said. "Don't get me wrong, I love what I do, and I'm so glad that my path took me where it did. I own my own business, for crying out

41

loud. But still, this is the first time I've been on a college campus. It's more beautiful than I ever imagined it would be."

Bob looked around, trying to see it through new eyes. He had done the college route, and it hadn't held the same excitement for him as he was sure it would have for someone like Debbie. But now, trying to view it from a fresh perspective, he started to see it. Maybe not fully, but a tiny glimpse.

"Would you like to walk around a bit?" he asked, glancing at his watch. "We have time before we need to go set up for the career fair. I didn't expect to get here so quickly."

"That's because, even though the GPS told you it would only take twenty minutes to get here from the hotel, you insisted it would take at least an hour," Debbie said with a small laugh.

His cheeks burned, but it was more because of what Debbie's laugh still did to him. "I bet we could even sit in on a class, if you'd like."

Debbie's eyes widened with what looked like both curiosity and anxiety. "I don't think I could do that. I'd be too intimidated. Maybe we could walk through a couple of the buildings, though?"

"Sure."

"What about you, Sandy?" Debbie asked. "Would you like to walk through a few buildings and see what they're like?"

Sandy's gaze was locked on a gigantic building made up entirely of windows. "How about if you guys go, and meet me at the library when you're done?" Her voice quivered with excitement. "I've never seen a library that big before," she half-whispered.

"That's because Amor's library is equivalent to a one-room schoolhouse," Debbie said with a laugh.

"You should take all the time you want," Bob said. "You can meet us at the student center when you're done, or we could swing by after the career fair. I'd hate to cut your time short."

Debbie threw a curious look Bob's way, and he tried to ignore it, and the way it made his breath shudder.

Sandy nodded but was already speed walking toward the library, like she was afraid he'd change his mind.

Debbie laughed, and she and Bob made their way down the sidewalk toward a cluster of buildings on the opposite side of campus.

Bob couldn't help but watch Debbie as they walked, her movements slow and purposeful, and yet there was a little spring to her step. He had been trying to forget for so long what she did to him. But now, it was all rushing back. She looked amazing in her pants suit, her hair loose and flowing down her back. But his attraction to her wasn't what brought the onslaught of emotion. It was how contagious her joy was. Just her presence made him happier.

He felt kind of guilty about it, because he didn't know if she was receiving any benefit in return. Maybe he was like a leech that got all the good stuff but didn't give anything back. That made him want to do better and be better, and so he was. He was a kinder and more adventurous version of himself when he was with Debbie. He was also more passionate. A lot more. Like, if 'normal Bob' was a one on the Richter scale, 'Bob with Debbie' was closing in on an eight. Maybe even a nine. He didn't want to give himself too much credit, though. It had everything to do with Debbie and almost nothing to do with him.

"Bob?"

He was pulled out of his thoughts, realizing that they were standing in front of one of the buildings, and Debbie was already halfway up the stairs.

"How about if we step into this one for a bit, and then we can go get the stuff to set up?" she asked, as if it wasn't the first time.

"Yeah, of course," he said, trying to bring himself back to the present. Back to reality, where Bob didn't have the luxury of pulling Debbie into his arms anymore. Not that he would have at that moment. He had a lot of anxiety about public displays of affection—something that had been the root cause of his and Debbie's relationship failure. He hadn't realized how big a problem it had been until it was too late. But she hadn't given him a chance to explain or the time he'd needed to overcome it. She'd just walked away, like the previous months hadn't meant anything to her.

As they walked in, a large sign announced that it was the business building.

"Hmm...it seemed a bit more impressive from the outside," Debbie said, seeming slightly disappointed. "It looks so..."

"Normal?"

Debbie glanced at him with a small smile. "Yeah. Normal."

Bob's gaze lingered on a bulletin board that hung on the wall. It had the schedule for each classroom, and in the room right next to them was an entrepreneurial business class. Perfect. He touched Debbie on the elbow to get her attention, and she spun toward him, as if he'd shocked her.

"Sorry, I didn't mean to startle you," he said, quickly taking a step back. "I just wondered if you'd like to catch the rest of this class with me. Just so you can get a glimpse of what it's like."

The idea seemed to make Debbie nervous and she scrunched up her nose. It was adorable.

"I don't know..."

Her hesitance surprised Bob. She was always the one to take charge and take the lead. "Come on, we'll just slip into the back. It's probably an auditorium-style classroom, so they won't even know we're there."

"We're allowed to do that?"

The question hung in the air as Bob realized she was actually asking, *Is it against the rules?*

It wasn't like Debbie to worry about whether something was against the rules—the 'precious' rules that governed Bob's life and dictated most of what he did. He'd never admit it, but he hated that part of himself. He hated his inflexibility, which was why Debbie had been so good for him. But now she was looking to the rules to give her an excuse to not go into this classroom. It went to show how anxious she really was.

"The worst that can happen is they ask us to leave," he finally said.

She tilted her head to one side, as if thinking. "All right."

With a nervous grin, she pulled open the door to the classroom, and Bob slipped in after her.

It was not an auditorium-style classroom, like Bob had predicted, but quite the opposite. It was small, with only about ten students and a man standing at the front who must have been the professor. He looked awfully young to be teaching.

Every head turned to look at them as Bob and Debbie stood awkwardly by the door. She looked like she wanted to back out, but Bob was in the way.

"Can I help you with something?" the professor asked. "We have about fifteen minutes left of class, but I can speak with you after."

"Actually, we were hoping to observe your class for a few minutes, but we didn't mean to interrupt," Bob said.

"We don't have to stay," Debbie said, her tone apologetic. Bob could tell she was embarrassed at having been noticed in such a public way, which perplexed him.

"No, please have a seat," the professor said, gesturing to a couple of empty seats in the back row.

Bob took a step forward, but Debbie didn't follow. He held her elbow gently and led her to the seats, trying to ignore the warmth he felt from the physical contact.

"What brings you to campus today?" the professor asked once they had sat down.

Bob waited for Debbie to take the lead, considering she was the Pied Piper of Amor and would have no trouble convincing all these young entrepreneurial students that Amor was where they wanted to be.

But she didn't speak. Instead, she looked down at her hands, which were folded on the desk in front of her.

"We're here for the career fair," Bob said. "We represent Amor, a small town that is exploding with growth due to the rise in popularity of space tourism."

The professor's eyes lit up. "Yes, I've been following that. And you are here recruiting?"

"Yes. My colleague, Debbie, owns her own business, and can attest to the opportunities that are just waiting for those who are brave enough to relocate down there. In fact, we have more job openings than we know what to do with."

"What kind of business do you own?" the professor asked, turning his attention to Debbie.

She seemed startled that he was addressing her, then said in a soft voice, "I have my own salon."

"Ooh, that's what I want to do," a young woman said from the front row. "Can you tell me what it's like?"

Debbie stared, then tilted her head slightly. "Yeah, okay."

"Why don't you come up here?" the professor asked, indicating a spot next to him in front of the class.

Debbie looked at Bob, uncertainty in her eyes.

"Go on," he whispered. "Tell them what it's like."

She slowly stood, then walked to the front of the class. "I have to be honest, I didn't go to college," she started. "I learned everything I needed to know from beauty school, books, and mentors in the business."

"Learning is learning, no matter where you gain the knowledge," the professor said, giving her an encouraging smile.

That seemed to boost her confidence a little, because when she spoke next, her voice rose in volume, and it was firmer than it had been. "If you want to own your own business, whether it is a salon or a comic book store, or whatever else you are passionate about, what matters is that you pay attention to trends and make sure you are providing what the customers want." She paused. "Now that I think about it, you may want to think about opening up a comic book store, because you would have no competition. Amor doesn't currently have one, and I'm not sure the kids down there have ever read one."

That elicited a few chuckles.

"Because you are your own boss, you can pay yourself whatever you want, right?" one of the students asked.

"Sure," Debbie said. "When I first started out, I made about a dollar an hour. I was living the high life."

A few of the students gaped, like they weren't sure if she was kidding or not.

"Don't forget, you're putting in a lot of time and money before you've even opened the doors. And then there's the problem of not having any customers at first, and having to earn their trust. You probably won't be able to hire an accountant or a marketing manager, so you'll need to learn all that too."

Silence followed her words, and it seemed that she had managed to convince everyone in the room to change their plans for the future.

"But," she said, holding up a finger, "if you can make it through all that and weather the storm, you will have the freedom to live the life you've always dreamed of. I was in the right place at the right time, and I am able to take advantage of the tourism industry that is exploding in Amor. But I wouldn't be having the success I am if I hadn't moved locations and started offering new services that I thought the tourists would enjoy. Hard work and adaptability will take you far and will reward you far beyond what you thought possible. But it takes patience, perseverance, and the ability to learn from your mistakes and initial failures."

Her final words rejuvenated the class, and they began clapping, a new energy having replaced the fear that had permeated the room.

"I couldn't have said it better myself," the professor said. "Class is over, but make sure you visit the career fair to meet with people like Debbie."

"I'm glad you stopped by," the professor said as Bob and Debbie moved to follow the students out. "There is nothing like having someone with real-world experience to drive home the principles I've been trying to hammer into their heads all semester."

"Thank you for having us," Debbie said, wearing a grin. "I think I would have liked college."

"I think you would have too," the professor said. "But don't feel like you missed out. It's not for everyone, and you've done beautifully without it."

Debbie's smile didn't wane as they stepped out into the sunlight and made their way back to Bob's car, where their supplies were. She looked so happy, and it lit up everything about her. She was naturally an optimistic person, but this seemed different.

"What happened in there?" Bob asked.

"What do you mean?" Debbie asked, leaping over a crack in the sidewalk.

How could he word this so it didn't come across as offensive? "You're usually the fearless one. There is nothing you won't do, no one you won't approach. So, what happened in there?"

Debbie's smile slipped and was replaced by a thoughtful crinkling of her brow. She hesitated before saying, "I didn't think I belonged in a place like this. I didn't think I should pretend that I was smart enough to sit in a classroom and act like I was one of them." She paused, and her voice softened. "I didn't think I had anything to contribute."

Bob was astounded. Debbie, who was beautiful and talented and confident, doubted that she was good enough to be there. "I hope you see how wrong you were," he said. "You are incredibly talented and could run circles around these college folk."

Debbie's smile returned. "I don't know about circles, but I think I could hold my own."

"I know you could. But you're meant for bigger and greater things than thinking about what might have been."

Debbie glanced at him with a thoughtful look, the edge of her lips tilting up. She didn't say anything more as they reached the car and pulled out two boxes that held a sign, free pens, and brochures on how to apply for employment in Amor.

"Let's show these kids what they're missing out on," she said, her eyes lighting up.

As Bob followed Debbie into the student union building, he couldn't help but think about what *he* was missing out on—what he had been missing out on for the past two years.

Chapter Seven

Debbie couldn't believe it was only mid-afternoon and the career fair was already finished. The time had sped by as she had talked with students, asked them about their aspirations, and explained how working in Amor could help them reach their goals. She had loved it, and wondered if Zoe would have more assignments like this that she'd like to send Debbie on. She wouldn't mind one bit.

Bob had actually been more talkative with the students than she had anticipated and was able to connect with several of the more serious-minded students that didn't seem to trust that Debbie knew what she was talking about. She had to admit that she and Bob had made a great team, and at times she'd forgotten that they weren't on speaking terms. And even when she did remember, she found herself still wanting to share her excitement with him, and it seemed that he wanted her to. He kept saying things like how impressive she was, and that she was in her element.

But then it brought back all the old feelings—the ones that hurt because they reminded her that Bob wasn't hers to call her own. They were there on assignment. And that was all there was to it.

"Shall we see what kind of restaurants this place has?" Bob asked, folding up the sign and placing it in his box. "I've always wanted to try Thai food."

"Thai?" Debbie asked, incredulous. Bob was usually...safer in his preferences. But maybe that was because Amor didn't have what she would label as 'risky' options. Or maybe she didn't know Bob like she thought she did.

"Sure," he said. "I hear it's good."

"All right. Let's do Thai," she said, taking out her phone and doing a quick search. "There's a Thai restaurant just a couple streets away. Let's swing by the library and make sure Sandy is okay with that. I'd hate to send her over the edge because we introduced too much too soon, poor girl."

"I think she's stronger than you give her credit for," Bob said, shutting the trunk of the car and meeting her on the sidewalk. "Sure, she's had a rough go of it, but she's a fighter. I can tell."

Debbie didn't respond right away. She was interested in how Bob knew this, but wasn't sure if she should ask. When she and Bob were dating, they'd talked a lot. But Debbie now realized they'd never talked about the deep personal stuff. She knew next to nothing about his family or how he'd become who he was, and it made her want to delve into what made him tick.

They arrived at the library before she'd mustered up the courage to say anything, and the moment was gone.

"Should I just call and ask her to meet us out here?" Debbie asked.

"Might as well. This place looks huge. Once we go in, we might never find our way back out again."

Debbie laughed and rolled her eyes, but sneaked in a quick glance at Bob to double-check that he'd been joking. With him, she was never quite sure. But he was wearing a half-smile, thank goodness, and she pulled out her phone.

It went straight to voicemail.

"Either her phone is off or dead, or she doesn't have reception," Debbie said, slipping the phone back into her purse.

"I guess we better go in and rescue her, then," Bob said.

"Somehow, I doubt she needs rescuing," Debbie said. "Did you see how excited she was to spend time at the library? I have a feeling she's going to be disappointed when we finally find her."

"Just the same, a university library can be pretty intimidating."

Debbie didn't understand what Bob meant by that until they walked through the front doors and the building sprawled before them. She glanced at a board to their right that had a layout of the library and a small dot that said 'You are Here.'

"There's four levels in this place?" she yelped. "You're right, we're never going to find her."

"Before you get all pessimistic on me, let's go under the assumption that she doesn't have cell service, rather than her phone being dead. That means she could be downstairs. The basement level never has good reception."

Of course. She should have thought of that.

They took the elevator down and walked into a maze of bookshelves. The rows seemed to go on for miles, and Debbie shook her head in disbelief.

"I feel like we're in a bookworm's version of the Labyrinth, and the librarian is the Minotaur," she said.

The corner of Bob's mouth lifted into a faint smile. "Did you bring your ball of string?"

Debbie stared at him blankly. "My what?"

"String," Bob repeated. "In the story of the Minotaur, Ariadne gives Theseus a ball of string so he can find his way back out of the maze. He ties one end to the door, and after he slays the Minotaur in the farthest corner of the Labyrinth, he's able to follow the string back out again."

"So...like Hansel and Gretel," Debbie said as she started to walk down one of the aisles.

"Yeah, except Hansel and Gretel would have been better off with Theseus's string. At least then the birds wouldn't have eaten it, like they did the breadcrumbs."

"That's true. But Hansen and Gretel get sympathy points. They were only kids, not warriors. How would you have liked to stuff a witch into an oven, after facing your imminent death? Talk about traumatic. They must have been in therapy for years after that."

They reached the end of that row and were faced with the choice of left or right, but when Debbie was about to ask Bob his opinion, she realized he was laughing so hard that she couldn't even hear it.

"Uh...are you okay?" she asked. There had been a time or two she'd seen Bob laugh like this, but she had never expected to see it again.

His face had turned bright red, and he couldn't speak, but he nodded his head. He sucked in a long breath. "Oh man, I haven't found anything that funny since..." He turned away. "Well, since you."

Debbie's heart fluttered, but she willed herself to turn away. "I think we should turn right and move along the periphery. That way we can look down each of the aisles as we pass them."

Bob eyed her for a moment, like he wasn't sure what to make of her abrupt change of topic, but then said, "I think that's a brilliant idea."

Debbie didn't think it was brilliant, but she didn't want to diminish Bob's compliment either, so she remained silent. They walked past several couches where students seemed to be holding group study sessions, and Debbie found herself drawn into the excitement and tension she felt in the air.

When they rounded a corner, they nearly tripped over a tall stack of books.

"What in the world?" Debbie asked. "Who just leaves books in the middle of the floor?"

"Sorry, that was me," a small voice said. "All the tables and couches were taken. It seems that it's almost finals week and everyone has tests to study for."

Debbie looked behind the pile of books to find Sandy sitting against the wall with books laid out around her, open to various points.

"You look like you're studying for an upcoming exam as well," Debbie said, stepping around the books.

Sandy's eyes shone. "I've never seen so many books in one place. I couldn't decide on just one. And I knew that I'd never be back to this library, so I had to make my time here count."

"I think you can safely say, 'Mission accomplished.'"

"Are you hungry?" Bob asked, picking up one of the books and flipping through it. "We thought we'd try out some Thai food, if you're interested."

"We can go anywhere, though," Debbie added hurriedly. "We aren't set on one place."

Bob raised an eyebrow at her, but she gave a slight shake of her head. She didn't want Sandy to feel like she was holding them back.

"I actually just bought a sandwich at a vending machine they have down here," Sandy said. "If it's all the same to you, I'd like to stay for a while longer."

"Of course," Debbie said. "How about if we meet you outside in a couple of hours?"

"Sounds good," Sandy said, her attention turning back to the book on her lap.

Debbie turned to leave, but Bob stayed rooted in place.

"What do you mean you bought a sandwich from a vending machine?" he asked. "They have places you can eat on campus."

Sandy finished reading the page she was on, then glanced up. "I know. But I didn't want someone to think I was done with these books and put them all away."

"But...it came from a machine." Bob seemed to find the idea so troubling that he couldn't move on from it.

"Yes," Sandy said, either not noticing or not caring that Bob found it completely repulsive. "And it was delicious. Almost as good as the sandwiches at the diner."

Bob balked. "But it fell through a slot at the bottom of—"

"She gets the point," Debbie said, grabbing Bob's arm and steering him away. "She watched her sandwich fall, and then she pulled it out and ate it. And she loved it. It's okay."

"But—"

He didn't let it go until they had exited the library.

"Feel better now that we're back in the sunshine?" she asked.

"I guess," he grumbled. "It's still not right."

Debbie realized she was still holding onto Bob, and she quickly let go. "I'm sure it's nothing that a bit of Thai food can't cure."

He nodded slowly. "I think you're right." He seemed to brighten at the thought and asked, "Want to walk?"

She liked the idea of exploring the city on foot. That was how she always got around Amor, and it made her more comfortable when she was able to take things slowly. "I'd like that."

They walked in silence for several minutes before Debbie felt the need to speak, which she fought against at first. "You were really good today," she finally said. "You're better with people than you pretend to be."

Bob snorted. "I've heard what people say about me at the office."

"It's because you haven't given them a reason to think otherwise," Debbie said. "You like rules more than them, and it shows. But with those college kids today—you were awesome. You spoke to them in a way that made them really respond to you."

"That's because they were math and engineering geeks. They love procedure almost as much as I do."

"Did you always love following the rules, even as a kid?" Debbie asked. She imagined a little Bobby running around, enforcing the rules on the playground. She smiled at the thought.

Bob didn't answer right away, and actually seemed to be trying to avoid the question when they stopped in front of the restaurant. A long line snaked out the front door.

"Guess Thai food must be as delicious as I've heard," Bob said. "But do you think it's delicious enough to make the wait worth it?"

"Absolutely," Debbie said, also wanting to try out something more exotic than they could find in Amor.

They pushed their way through the crowd to where they placed their name on the waiting list and were told to return in an hour. After making their way back outside, they wandered down the sidewalk with an unspoken understanding that they'd continue walking until it was time for them to return for their dinner.

"You didn't answer my question," Debbie said.

"I know."

They were silent for another beat before Debbie asked, "Are you going to?"

"Probably not."

She chanced a glance at Bob and noticed that he was staring straight in front of him, his gait stiff. She decided not to push it. If there was something about his childhood that he didn't want to talk about, it wasn't her place to get him to. That was something that girlfriends did, and she no longer held that title. Maybe if she had tried getting to know him on a deeper level when she'd had the chance, things would have turned out differently. But how could she have when he was so hot and cold with her?

Bob spoke suddenly and his voice had a hard edge to it. "Why do women like the men who are rule breakers—the ones who are unpredictable and no good for them?"

Debbie was about to tell him that wasn't true, but she couldn't deny that she had known far more women who were excited by a man with a motorcycle than by a man who drove an eco-friendly Smart Car and was in bed by ten o'clock.

But then again, what was so bad about being a rule breaker?

"Let me ask you this," Debbie said. "Why did you date me? Aren't I the equivalent of an unpredictable rule breaker?"

She didn't know why she had brought up the past—that seemed like the worst thing she could have done in that moment. But it was true, wasn't it? She was the one who moved to the beat of a different drum, changed her hair color every other day, and didn't let others dictate what she could or couldn't do. Debbie was grateful every day for her salon, because she couldn't imagine having to answer to a boss. And she didn't think she was any worse off for it. In fact, she was proud of it.

Bob's head whipped toward Debbie, like he too was stunned by her words. "What?"

Now that the words were out, she was going to have to stand behind them. She met his gaze. "You heard me. I'm a rule breaker. I don't always make sure my doors are locked, and I take all the little shampoos and soaps from my hotel rooms—even the ones I didn't use. Does that make me less worthy to find my happily-ever-after than you?"

Bob's lips moved, but nothing came out. He finally sucked in a long breath and said, "No, of course not. But you're different. You're not at all like the type of people I'm talking about."

"How so?" Debbie demanded. "I've seen you criticize others for doing far less than what I do."

He stopped in the middle of the sidewalk and looked around, like he was nervous that people would overhear their conversation, which was getting louder by the moment. "Yes," he said in a low voice. "But I was in love with you, and that makes a big difference."

That was enough to leave Debbie's mouth hanging open. "Well, all right then," she said, spinning on her heel to walk back the way they had come. "I think we should see if our table is ready." She walked quickly back toward the restaurant. His admission of his love shouldn't have been as shocking as it had been. He had told her that he loved her when they were dating. But the reality of it seemed a stark contrast to what their relationship had dissolved into.

Bob called after her, "Debs, wait."

That was enough to stop her. She hadn't heard that nickname in a long time, and hearing it come from his lips—it sent her stomach flipping end over end.

"What?" she asked when he drew near.

Now that she was looking at him, giving him the chance to say something, he seemed to be all tongue-tied, and nothing came out. His lips kept parting, like he might speak, but then would close again.

"I don't claim to understand you," Debbie said with a long sigh, when it became apparent that she would need to be the one to speak. "You can be the most amazing person, and yet you refuse to show that side to people. Instead, you hide behind your rules and procedures. If you don't want to tell me why, that's fine. That's your burden to carry. I lost the right to know when we broke up. But can we just leave it at that and enjoy our dinner tonight? I've had a really nice day, and I want it to end on a good note."

Bob looked down at the pavement for a moment, and then in lieu of an answer, he reached down and took Debbie's hand in his.

She froze, not sure what was happening. He was taking her hand. In public. For the first time, ever.

His gaze finally met hers and he said, "I'm sorry. I would never want to be the cause of ruining your night."

She looked away from the sincerity she saw in his eyes. Why couldn't he be this way all the time? Debbie already knew the answer. It was because they weren't in Amor. If they knew any of these people walking past, it would be a different story. She knew he wouldn't have taken her hand.

She blinked back a couple of tears as they turned to walk back to the restaurant, but she didn't remove her hand from his. Her tears weren't from sadness, but yearning. Why couldn't he have seen what a good thing they had going?

But as she felt his fingers tighten around hers, she thought that even though they couldn't go back in time and change things, maybe she could hold onto this moment for just a little longer.

Chapter Eight

Bob drove, trying to ignore the tingling he still felt in his fingers from holding Debbie's hand the previous evening. He still couldn't believe that he had done it, but he didn't regret it. She hadn't pulled away, and that said something. He didn't know what that said yet, but a glimmer of hope had been left behind, even after she had removed her hand from his at the restaurant.

Bob couldn't remember a time he'd enjoyed dinner more. Of course, he hadn't realized that Thai spice was very different from Mexican spice, so when he had ordered his meal extra hot—well, he went through several glasses of water before the night was through. What was more embarrassing was the sweat that had beaded along his forehead as he worked his way through his food. It was delicious, though, and the Thai food was just another part of the night that he didn't regret.

A quick glance told him that Debbie was still awake in the passenger seat, though she was very quiet. Quieter than usual for her, even with how weird things had been between them. He had pretended not to notice when she asked Sandy if she'd like a turn in the front seat as they drove the three hours to their next destination. She'd declined, and Debbie had looked torn as she finally relented and slid into the front seat.

Did she not still feel the pressure of his hand in hers like he did? Or maybe she was trying to forget it.

An ache welled in his chest. He knew that he wasn't the ideal boyfriend. He didn't have much practice and was clueless most of the time, but hadn't she known how much he had cared for her? Hadn't she caught just a glimpse of that last night?

It didn't seem like it. Whatever special thing they had shared, it was gone, and it wasn't coming back.

Bob threw another glance Debbie's way, but she continued to look out her window. He wondered if she really found the rolling desert that interesting, or if she was purposely avoiding him.

He already knew the answer.

With a silent sigh, he faced forward, but just as he did, he noticed an animal loping across the freeway, right in the path of the car. Bob simultaneously glanced in the rearview mirror to make sure no one was behind him and braked as quickly as he could, without throwing all of them through the windshield. It did no good. He couldn't stop in time, and the car still hit the animal.

Bob pulled the car over to the shoulder of the road and jumped out. It turned out the animal was a skunk, and though it lay in the middle of the road, it wasn't dead. Relief rushed through Bob. The animal's head lifted slightly, but it didn't seem able to move.

"No, no, no, no," he said.

"Leave it alone," Debbie said, jumping out of the car. "We'll call wildlife protection. They can come deal with it."

"Another car will run over it before they get here," Bob said, glancing anxiously down the road. It was only a matter of time before a large semi-truck came lumbering this way. And the driver wouldn't even feel the bump as he drove over the poor animal.

Making up his mind, he popped the trunk of his car and pulled out the box that held their career fair supplies. He dumped them out, then grabbed a spare blanket he kept in case of emergencies.

He lined the box with the blanket, then checked to make sure no cars were coming.

"This is a bad idea," Sandy said as she too jumped out of the car. Fear laced her words. "When I agreed with my therapist that coming on this trip was a good idea, he said that you were the safest person to do this with, Bob. He said you didn't take risks. You don't even have gloves. What if that skunk has rabies?"

Guilt gnawed at Bob, but leaving this animal here to die was something he couldn't do. With or without rabies. He was the reason it was injured. Checking once more to make sure there weren't any cars coming from the horizon, he sprinted into the road, then placed one hand under the skunk's head and the other under its body. He knew the skunk could lash out at him, trying to protect itself from further injury.

Bob braced himself to be bitten, but the skunk merely looked at him, its body limp. He placed the skunk in the box and covered everything but its head with the blanket, then ran back out of the road. He placed the box on the ground next to the car, panting.

Sandy ran up to him and flung her arms around his neck. "You have to promise me you'll never do anything like that again," she said into his shoulder. She stepped back. "I can't handle it." Her complexion was pale, and it sent a new wave of guilt through Bob.

He wanted to give Sandy her promise to help ease her fears. But if they came across the situation again, he knew he'd have to respond the same way he just had. "Let's just hope we don't hit any more animals on this journey."

Sandy stared at him, then turned and got back in the car.

Debbie walked up and picked up the box. She looked from the skunk to Bob.

He dropped his gaze to the ground and simply said, "I couldn't let it die."

She was silent for a moment, then with a small smile, said, "I know." She walked to her side of the car. "I'll hold the box on my lap, and you can find the nearest wildlife rehabilitation center."

Bob watched her, stunned at how beautifully she was handling the situation.

"You coming?" she asked, a corner of her mouth lifting, as if it were teasing him.

"Oh, yeah." He slid into his seat and pulled up the GPS. "It looks like there is one an hour away, which is pretty fortunate. There are only two in the whole state."

For the whole way there, Bob couldn't help but steal glances at the box and ask, "Is it still alive?"

"Yes," Debbie patiently answered.

"How do you know?"

"Because it's looking at me."

Then Sandy piped up from the back seat. "Is it looking at you in a way that says it wants to eat you?"

"Skunks don't eat people," Debbie answered.

"But that one might. At the very least, it might spray you, which is almost as bad as being eaten."

It was a relief when they pulled into the rehabilitation center. As soon as they pulled up, a woman with a bird sitting on her shoulder walked out of the building. The bird's wing was bandaged, and it seemed content to just ride for the time being.

Bob stepped out of the car and walked around to open Debbie's door for her.

"Good morning," the woman said, approaching the car. "You have something for us?"

"Yes," Bob said, lifting the box from Debbie's lap and showing the woman what was inside.

The woman whistled. "Do you realize how lucky you are? You are the third person to bring in a skunk this week, and you are the only one that hasn't been bitten or sprayed." She paused and looked Bob over. "You weren't, were you?"

"No," he assured her. "I hit it with my car on the freeway."

"Well, that is very noble of you to bring it in, but in the future, we advise not risking doing it yourself, but calling us instead."

"That's what I told him," Debbie said from the front seat.

The woman laughed. "Yes, well, men don't always listen, do they?"

"You got that right," Debbie mumbled.

Bob fought the annoyance he felt toward Debbie's remark. He'd done the right thing. He knew he had.

"I'll take her from you now," the woman said, taking the box from Bob, which left him feeling strangely empty.

"How do you know it's a girl?" he asked.

"I don't," the woman said, "but the males tend to be a little bit larger, so I'm assuming." She turned to take the skunk inside. "Thanks again."

"Wait," Bob said. The woman glanced back over her shoulder. "Can we watch? You know, make sure she will be all right?"

The woman turned to face him but shook her head. "I'm afraid that our hospital is off-limits to visitors. I'm sorry." She paused. "But you could take a short tour of a few of our outdoor enclosures, if you'd like. I could have a volunteer take you around."

Bob almost said yes right away, but then realized he should probably make sure it was okay with Sandy and Debbie. "Would you like to?" he asked them.

Sandy stepped out of the car and threw nervous glances toward the rehabilitation center. "They are all enclosed? No wild animals are wandering around?"

"No animals are wandering around," the woman assured her. "We try to make their enclosures large and as similar to their natural habitat as possible, to help them feel comfortable while here."

Sandy paused before giving a hesitant nod. "All right."

"I'll send someone out," the woman said as she carried the skunk into the building.

A few minutes later, a young man walked out. He wore a polo shirt with the rehabilitation center's logo embroidered on it. "You the folks looking for a tour?"

"Yes," Bob answered.

The man held out a hand and Bob shook it. "I'm David."

"I'm Bob, and this is Sandy and Debbie."

David nodded in greeting to both women, but his gaze lingered on Sandy. She met his gaze and blushed.

After an awkward moment, Bob asked, "What kind of animals do you have here?"

It took another moment for David to answer the question, but he finally turned and motioned for them to follow him. "We have just about everything you could think of— rattlesnakes, jackrabbits, coyotes. We even have a mountain lion."

"Mountain lion?" Sandy squeaked. "Out in the desert?"

"They don't prefer it, of course," David said, glancing back. "But a home range for a lion can be over a hundred square miles, which can include a broad range of habitats, especially in New Mexico."

"Oh." She looked around nervously, like she expected one to jump out at her.

They rounded the corner of the building and were met with a desert landscape dotted with large cages.

"We don't have time to visit every animal, but I can show you a few," David said. "I'll save the lion for last." He moved over to a dirt path that they followed for a couple of minutes.

"How can lions find enough of what they need out here in the wild?" Bob asked, noting the barren landscape.

"They can survive longer than you'd expect without water, and there is plenty of food. They'll eat jackrabbits, skunks, and other things like that. The desert isn't as dead as it appears at first glance."

Bob knew that, of course, but to imagine something like a mountain lion surviving out here was different. Although, if a coyote could, why not a lion?

"Here we have Susan," David said, stopping. "She's our resident skunk."

Sandy bent down to get a closer look. "Oh," she breathed. "I never thought I'd say this about a skunk, but she's beautiful."

"You didn't say that about the one I just rescued," Bob said, but no one paid him any attention.

"They are some of the most underappreciated creatures," David said, stooping next to her. "Not only do they eat pesky insects and rodents, but did you know they are immune to snake venom? They'll actually eat poisonous snakes, like rattlesnakes."

"That's amazing," Sandy said, her eyes widening.

"We just brought in a skunk," Bob said, a little louder, purposely interrupting their little moment. He didn't like how close David was to Sandy. She was naive to how the world worked, and Bob was afraid that David would be all too willing to explain it to her.

David glanced back at Bob. "Yes, I saw. Susan will be glad to have a friend. She's been here longer than we expected, and she's seemed a bit lonely as of late." He turned back to Sandy and seemed to inch closer to her. "Now, if you'll notice her front claws—"

"Maybe we can move on to the next animal," Bob said, interrupting them again.

"What is your problem?" Debbie whispered, elbowing him. "Leave them alone."

Bob balked. "Don't you see what's happening here?"

Debbie glanced toward David and Sandy, then placed a hand on Bob's back and led him further down the path. He tried to ignore the shocks of excitement that radiated from where she touched. They took a left turn and walked for another minute more.

"Yes," she finally said. "I see what's happening here. After all these years that Sandy has had to suffer being set up on countless dates by her mother, with none of the men remotely interested in Sandy, she has finally attracted the attention of a man on her own. And you are not going to ruin that for her."

"But we don't know anything about him," Bob protested.

"We do know one thing," Debbie said. Her arm dropped to her side and she took a step away, as if she'd suddenly realized that she had still been touching him.

"His name."

"Okay, two things."

Bob racked his brain but couldn't think of anything else. They knew nothing about this guy, and that was the problem.

She must have sensed his hopelessness because she chuckled and said, "He's a volunteer at a wildlife rehabilitation center."

Oh, right. "So?"

"Are all men this clueless?" she asked with raised eyebrows. "Or are you purposely not wanting to see him as a good guy?"

Probably both, but Bob wouldn't admit it. Instead, he raised one shoulder and gave her the concession she was looking for. "Fine. He's probably not a terrible person if he's volunteering here." He turned to the nearest enclosure and saw that it housed a coyote with its paw bandaged. He wished he could live somewhere like this, doing nothing but taking care of these animals all day. He wondered if there were any job openings.

"There's nothing more attractive than a man who takes care of injured animals," Debbie said. "With the way David was talking about that skunk, Sandy's probably already in love with him."

"*Nothing* is more attractive than that?" Bob asked, skeptical. What about all those tough guys he'd been competing with for years? They hadn't gotten the girl by feeding a sick skunk.

"It's how I first met you," Debbie said.

Bob froze. He remembered the day well. Until then, he'd heard of Debbie, but they had never met. She had just returned to Amor after attending cosmetology school and had come into the small animal shelter Bob volunteered at, looking for a pet.

He had been sitting on the floor, trying to get an injured rabbit to drink from a bottle. It hadn't eaten for days and he was afraid that if it didn't start soon, it wouldn't make it through the night.

A woman with purple dreadlocks had seemed to appear out of nowhere and sat on the floor next to him. "Is this one available to adopt?" she'd asked.

"You don't want this one," he'd said. "It probably won't survive more than a couple days. A week at the most."

"Maybe, but I bet it would prefer living its last days at my place than in a cage here."

That had made Bob look at Debbie—really look at her—for the first time. She had taken the rabbit home and helped nurse it back to health. It seemed the change of scenery had been what it needed, and it had lived for another five years.

Bob and Debbie hadn't started dating right away, but Debbie had made sure to go out of her way to say hello to him whenever she saw him around town.

"We should probably get going," Bob said, shaking himself from the memory. "Don't want to get to the hotel too late." He turned away from the coyote and saw that Debbie was staring at him with an awed look about her. He shifted nervously. "What?"

"I can't believe it took me this long to see it," she said, shaking her head. "It explains everything."

Now she was really making him nervous. "I don't know what you're talking about." And he didn't want to know. He moved to walk past her, but she placed a hand on his arm.

"People in Amor think you don't have empathy. But it isn't that at all. You have too much of it."

Bob paused, a flood of emotions sweeping through him. "Like I said," he managed to say. "I don't know what you're talking about."

"Yes, I do," Debbie said, her eyes shining like she had just solved the world's most challenging puzzle. "Your desire to protect Sandy from David, saving that skunk on the freeway—even when you accused Zoe's husband of being a terrorist because he hadn't made an official appointment with the mayor—it all comes down to your desire to protect those around you."

"In my defense, it was before Zoe started dating Stephen, and it was my first time meeting him."

"You're missing the point," Debbie said impatiently.

"Okay, fine," Bob said, not liking that she had hit the nail on the head. "Congratulations, you figured me out. Can we go now?"

"Sure," Debbie said, though she didn't move to leave. "But I have one more question. Why do you keep others from seeing who you really are? What are you afraid of?"

Bob knew what she was asking, but that wasn't a direction he wanted this conversation to take. He hadn't allowed the subject of his childhood to come up when they were dating, and he certainly wasn't going to let it now.

"Like I said, time to go," he said, shaking Debbie's hand off his arm.

She didn't try to stop him as he walked quickly away, but the words that followed him had the desired effect. "Who hurt you?"

Chapter Nine

Debbie had seen the flash of pain in Bob's eyes when she'd realized that all his rigid behaviors weren't because he loved rules and regulations, but because he needed the protection that the rules gave him. Why hadn't she noticed it before?

Bob paused mid-step, and it gave Debbie the courage to push on.

"I don't know who hurt you," she called after him. "But I'm not that person. And neither is David."

"You think I don't know that?" Bob asked, turning to face her. "You think I like being like this?" He gestured from his head to his feet. "I know what people say about me. Heck, sometimes I'm there when they say it."

Debbie's heart ached for him and she took a step forward. "There's nothing wrong with you. You're just misunderstood."

"You're wrong," Bob said, shaking his head fiercely. "There is something wrong with me. There is a lot wrong with me. I'm broken, and I can't be fixed."

He turned away and Debbie could tell he was about to rush off, but she couldn't let him do that. She wanted him to know that he wasn't alone, and she was there for him. Debbie quickened her steps and put herself in his path.

"You are not broken," she said with a fierceness that surprised both of them. "Rules and laws protect us, and you do the same thing. What's wrong with that?"

The pain in Bob's eyes deepened. He reached out, like he wanted to touch her, but he hesitated. "Everything," he said softly. "People don't want to be protected. They want to be liked and accepted. And I don't know how to do that."

"You seemed to do just fine with me," Debbie said, taking his hand and guiding it to her cheek. He didn't pull back this time, and his hand rested against her skin, its warmth spreading through Debbie until it reached her toes. It made her breath catch, and in that moment, she wanted nothing more than for things to go back to how they'd been.

"You made it easy," he murmured. It was another moment before he allowed his hand to drop, and Debbie immediately missed his touch. His posture drooped, and he collapsed onto a large rock that lined the path. "Have you ever been in an environment that is so chaotic and unpredictable that you end up relying on yourself because at least then you'll know what to expect?"

Debbie wanted to empathize, but no, she didn't know the feeling. She wished she did, though, if for no other reason than to know how to help Bob. "I'm sorry," she said. "I've always been independent, but it's because that's what I needed, not what was forced upon me."

Bob gave a nod so small that Debbie doubted she would have even noticed if she hadn't been watching him so closely. He stayed silent and seemed to have retreated further into himself.

"Is that what happened to you?" she asked, sitting on a rock adjacent to his.

It was another minute before Bob spoke. "My parents. They thought that giving my brothers and me our freedom would help us find who we were 'meant to be.'" He used air quotes around the last part. "They always told us that we needed space to find our true passion. I could come home at any time I wanted and do whatever I felt like. There were no expectations."

"Sounds like every kid's dream," Debbie said.

"Kids don't know what's good for them."

He had a point.

"You didn't like all that freedom?" she asked, urging him to continue. This was a side of Bob he'd never allowed her to see, and she was afraid that if he stopped now, he'd never tell her the rest of the story.

Bob gave a slight shake of his head. "Maybe it's fine for some. One of my brothers turned out okay. He spent all his time playing football and he's on a team with the NFL now. Can't remember which one; I don't really follow that kind of stuff."

"What about your other brother?"

"Jail, the last time I heard. It turned out that his passion was grand theft auto. Not the video game."

Debbie watched Bob. In place of the confident man she knew, a sad, scared kid sat in his place. "What was your passion?"

"Survival, at first," he said, his gaze on the ground.

Debbie's breathing stalled. "Survival?"

Bob's gaze met hers. "Sure. No rules, remember? That went for my parents too. Sometimes my mom made dinner, but most of the time we were on our own. My brothers were happy eating corn dogs or cereal for every meal, but I taught myself how to cook. As I discovered after I ran away, that was one of the best things I could have done for myself."

"Wait...what?" Debbie stared. There was no way that Bob was a runaway. Not the man she'd gotten to know over the years. No one who knew him would believe that.

Bob looked off into the distance. His mouth opened like he was going to tell her more, but he remained quiet.

"You can't say something like that and then leave me hanging," Debbie said, inching closer to Bob.

He gave her a side glance. "I already said more than I should have."

"This is something that is really important and helped shape who you are," Debbie said. "I'd like to know more."

Bob looked away. "Why, so you can be the center of the town gossip?"

Debbie's gut felt like it had been sliced open, and she recoiled. "How can you say something like that?"

"That's how our town works, isn't it? Gossip is like currency there, and you'd be a millionaire. You'd be the one who finally cracked Bob."

Tears stung her eyes and she stood. "When we were dating, you asked me not to tell anyone until you were ready. I didn't like it, but I kept my promise. No one knew. And to accuse me of anything less means you don't know me."

Debbie sprang up and walked away so quickly, she only caught a glimpse of the guilt that shadowed Bob's face.

"Wait," he said. His voice sounded like it was caught in his throat, struggling to escape.

But there was something else in his voice. Something that made Debbie stop. It had a touch of desperation, but it was more than that.

She turned.

Bob had stood and he took a step toward Debbie. With hesitation, he said, "My parents brought home a rabbit when I was a teenager. They had found it along the road with an injured leg.

Despite their lax parenting practices, they had good hearts. They said it was mine and my brothers' responsibilities to take care of it. I think that's the only thing they had ever asked of us."

Debbie took a step toward Bob.

He looked her in the eyes and seemed to hold his breath for a moment, then continued. "We took turns, or we were supposed to. The brother just older than me, he at least made sure it had food and was in its cage at night." He took another step forward. "I loved that rabbit. Gilbert. That was what I named him. I would hold him as often as I could, stroking his ears. He seemed to be the only one around who wanted to hear what I had to say."

"What happened?" Debbie asked.

Bob took another step. He was so close now that all Debbie had to do was shift her weight and her arm would brush his. "My eldest brother, the car thief, didn't care about Gilbert. Or anyone else, for that matter. One night after we'd had the rabbit for a few weeks and his leg was doing better, my mom asked my brother to go out and make sure Gilbert was in his hutch for the night. Later, when she asked my brother about it, he said he had done it, but he hadn't." Bob paused and sucked in a slow breath. "I went out to check on Gilbert the next morning, but instead found pieces of him in the neighbor's yard. Right next to their dog kennel."

Debbie's hand flew to her mouth. "Oh, I'm so sorry."

Bob's eyes held shadows and he frowned. "My parents didn't discipline my brother, but instead talked about the circle of life." He paused and reached out, taking Debbie's hand in his. Her breath hitched. "I couldn't stay there anymore."

"How old were you?" she said, her voice barely above a whisper.

"Fifteen."

Her eyes widened. "That's so young. When you left, did you drop out of school?"

Bob rubbed his thumb over her knuckles, sending chills down her spine. "I wasn't that dumb. I knew how important an education was. I had a friend who left the back door to his family's guest house unlocked for me and I'd sneak in there. It hadn't been used for years and the dust was an inch thick, but for me, it was a refuge."

Debbie squeezed his hand, hoping he realized it was her way of telling him that she was there for him—that he could trust her. "Didn't your parents notice?"

"At the time, I wasn't sure. Later I found out that they had been worried, at first, because I was never home later than eight o'clock, despite their lack of curfew. But then they had called the school, and when they heard I hadn't missed any classes, they attributed my disappearance to 'following my own path.' They said that I was a good kid with my head on my shoulders, and they trusted me."

Debbie was both appalled and impressed. He must have been an exceptional son for them to not worry about their fifteen-year-old making his own way through the world. Of course, they may have reacted the same way if Bob's brothers had run away from home, or as his parents put it, followed their passion.

"That's why you volunteer at the animal shelter back home," she said, thinking back to when she'd first seen him on the ground, stroking the rabbit that later became hers. He had seemed so at peace with the little animal. It was in that very first moment of meeting him that she had fallen in love with Bob.

"Yes."

Bob still held her hand, and Debbie felt a pull of attraction, begging her to close the gap between them. Their gazes locked and she shifted her weight, ready to give in. But then she stopped herself at the last second. It was the rabbit scenario all over again. Just because the man had a tragic past and a soft spot for cute, furry animals didn't mean she needed to throw herself at him, like she had when they had dated. It was even harder to step away this time, now that he was dressed down in his jeans and still sported his new facial hair. She wondered if not shaving was Bob's way of 'sticking it to the man' and showing how little he had wanted to come on this trip. It didn't seem like something Bob would do, but then again, it turned out there was a lot about him she didn't know.

With a burst of resolve, Debbie slid her hand from his and stepped away. "Thank you. For trusting me," she said. "I won't tell anyone."

"I know," Bob said with a small smile. She could see in his eyes that he really did know she was telling the truth. They were clear and open—and happy. "I haven't told anyone that story, and it feels good to finally share the burden."

An onslaught of emotions hit Debbie all at once. She couldn't define all of them, but she was able to isolate the pride that comes when a person has become a trusted confidante. It was quickly followed by longing. Why couldn't Bob have shared these things when they were dating? Would things go back to normal when they returned to Amor, now that she knew his secret? Or did this make them something more than they had been?

"Bob...I—" Debbie didn't know how she was going to finish that sentence, but it turned out that she didn't need to. She was still struggling to find the words when Bob closed the gap between them and pulled her close.

"I can't believe I let you walk away," he whispered, entwining his fingers with her hair. "Can you ever forgive me?" His face was inches from hers, his eyes pleading.

"I forgave you a long time ago," she said, her voice matching the softness of his. "But that doesn't mean I'm ready for you to walk back into my life." Despite her words, she wrapped her arms around his waist, and her desire for what they had shared intensified. The emotions that had hit her hard earlier had never dissipated, and now that they had a fuse, they exploded. Any rational thought that she still clung to was shoved aside, no longer relevant.

"I'm not ready for that either," Bob said, though his words were muffled by his and Debbie's lips colliding. His were softer than she remembered, and their lips moved in a frantic dance as they attempted to make up for lost time.

Despite the very little space between Bob and Debbie, they struggled to pull the other closer, hands entangled with hair, their breath coming out ragged.

"At least we both know that this is a terrible idea," Debbie breathed out as his kisses traveled along her jawline, making her release an involuntary and completely embarrassing groan.

"Yes, terrible," he agreed, before nibbling on her bottom lip, which made her wish there was something she could push him up against.

Debbie relished the scratch of Bob's facial hair against her cheek and she let her inhibitions go. She couldn't imagine regretting something as amazing as what she was feeling in that moment.

Whatever the consequences, this was totally worth it.

Chapter Ten

B ob stole a glance at Debbie as they drove. She was already looking at him, and she didn't seem embarrassed at having been caught doing so. Instead, she held his gaze for an extra beat, then casually turned to look out her window.

He turned his own gaze back to the road in front of them, not sure what to make of all this. He was obviously still very much in love with Debbie, but did she return his feelings? Or did she consider their kiss a moment of weakness? Just the thought of it made his cheeks warm with the desire for an encore performance. Bob already knew that Debbie was a fantastic kisser, but that had been something else entirely. They hadn't come up for air until they had heard their names being called from the next path. They had pulled apart just in time, but David had given them a look like he knew what they had been up to.

Bob shook his head, trying to clear those thoughts. He needed to focus on the career fair they'd be attending the next day. Not that he cared about it—at all. But it would give him something to think about and get his mind off how amazing Debbie's lips tasted and—

"How long until we're there?" Sandy asked from the back seat. She leaned forward and placed her head between the front seats.

Bob started at the interruption and hoped the content of his thoughts hadn't been obvious. "Only about forty-five minutes."

Sandy nodded and settled back in her seat.

Despite his efforts, Bob's thoughts immediately jumped back to where they had left off. He threw a side glance Debbie's way. He didn't just want to spend a week with her. He wanted to spend forever with her. Bob wanted to do the things that normal couples did—the things he hadn't been able to do before. Maybe he'd even take her to one of the new fancy restaurants that had moved into their town. The ones he had sworn off. He thought she'd like that.

But he needed more time to figure out how he was going to achieve all that. Because once they arrived back in Amor—he hoped things wouldn't go back to normal, but he knew they would. Yes, he and Debbie had kissed, but he knew from experience that that wasn't enough to fix what had pushed them apart.

Change.

That was what needed to happen.

Bob knew he had been the problem last time, and the only way to fix things was for him to change. But how did one go about transforming oneself into a completely different person? That was what Debbie needed, wasn't it? Someone who was like Bob—but not him. Not the man who dotted every i and crossed every t, avoiding risk at all costs. She needed someone who could walk down the streets of Amor and hold her hand, with people watching. Maybe even kiss her.

He would become the person Debbie wanted him to be. And he needed to start immediately.

WHEN BOB WOKE UP IN his hotel room, it seemed brighter than usual. He'd have to make sure he didn't stay in this hotel again if they couldn't even put up decent curtains that could keep out the early morning light.

Bob must have slept well, because he felt more refreshed than usual. He stretched, cracking his back in the process, then reached for his phone to begin his usual routine. The first thing he always did was look over the to-do list he had made the previous evening. It helped keep him organized and stress-free.

Except, his phone wasn't on the nightstand. He sat up. Had he accidentally knocked it to the floor? After a thorough search, including under the bed, his phone was still nowhere to be found. It wasn't until his bladder insisted he give up and use the bathroom that he discovered his phone shoved under a tissue box on the bathroom counter. It was turned off.

Something definitely wasn't right.

Bob pushed the power button and opened the app on his phone where he kept his lists, but then frowned. There wasn't one for that day. Had he not saved it? If so, that would be a first. He was still trying to figure out what could have happened when a knock sounded on the door.

Who would that be? It was too early for housekeeping, and he would certainly be awake before Debbie or Sandy. Well, whoever it was, if this was an emergency, he didn't want his internal debate to put him, and whoever was in the hallway, in danger.

It only took four steps for Bob to cross the room. He quickly unlocked the door and flung it open.

On the other side stood Debbie and Sandy, both dressed in business suits. They stepped backward and both women seemed shocked at seeing him, as if they hadn't just been pounding on his door.

"What's wrong? Has something happened?" he asked, searching their expressions.

Debbie recovered first and looked down. "We were worried about you, but it looks like everything is fine." When she glanced back up at Bob, her cheeks flushed.

Sandy grinned. "From where I'm standing, everything is more than fine."

Seeing him in his pajamas must have been more than Debbie could handle, because she could barely look at him. They were plaid flannel, though. It wasn't like he was wearing anything scandalous. Except, when he reached to scratch an itch on his arm, his fingers met with bare skin. Looking down, he realized he wasn't wearing a shirt.

How had that happened?

He always wore a shirt to bed.

Except, apparently, last night.

Feeling very exposed, Bob backed up into his room. "I'll be back."

Sandy didn't bother stifling her giggle, and as he shut the door, she called out, "Who would have known there were muscles under all those starched shirts?"

Bob leaned against the door. First his phone, then the to-do list, and now he was missing a shirt? On a hunch, he grabbed his phone and looked at the time.

"Ten o'clock?" he yelped. The career fair would be starting in thirty minutes. He had wanted to be there at least an hour early, considering he wasn't familiar with the campus. How had he slept in? No wonder the sun had seemed so bright this morning.

And then it all came back to him.

His determination to win Debbie back. To be someone she wanted to be with, and not just for this trip.

Bob must have been exhausted and not in his right mind, because in a moment of brave resolve, he had determined to do everything opposite to how he would normally do it. That meant skipping his to-do list and just going with the flow, as well as turning off his alarm—though he had turned it on and off three times before he had finally needed to hide it away in the bathroom, where he couldn't see it. And apparently it had also included not wearing a shirt to bed.

Bob groaned as he grabbed his suit. He got dressed in record time, shoved his wallet and keys in his pocket, and hurried out the door.

Debbie and Sandy still stood there, waiting.

"Breakfast is closed," Debbie said, "but I grabbed you something on my way out." She held out a muffin that was large enough to be three muffins shoved together. "Hope you like blueberry."

"Love it," Bob said, taking it from her. "And thank you."

Her bright blue eyes were all it took for his determination to return. This vibrant and amazing woman was worth fighting for. Bob smiled as he pulled at a corner of his shirt so that it stuck out.

"We were so worried," Sandy said as they hurried down the hall. "Debbie was running around demanding to know if anyone had seen you."

"Really?" he asked, glancing at her.

"I tried calling you several times, and it always went straight to voicemail," Debbie said, not looking his way. It almost seemed like she was purposely keeping her gaze forward. "I've never gotten your voicemail. Ever."

Guilt gnawed at Bob. "I'm sorry about that. I couldn't find my phone this morning. It seems that it had been turned off last night."

"That explains you sleeping in," Sandy said. "Debbie said you'd never risk being late to work." She looked Bob over as they waited for the elevator. "That also explains your growing beard."

"Huh?" Bob rubbed a hand over his face. His beard was getting longer than he was comfortable with, and he had meant to shave. Until that morning, he hadn't realized how much he relied on his routine. Now everything was turned upside down, and he didn't like it.

"What's the plan?" Debbie asked as they rode the elevator down.

He reached for his phone, but then realized it wouldn't help him. There was no plan. "Uh...go set up at the career fair."

"O-kay," she said, raising an eyebrow. "But what do you need me to do when we get there? Are we going to use the video montage we used at the last school? Last night you said you'd call your contact at the university and check if this place has an outlet we can use."

Oh. Yeah, Bob hadn't done that. He hadn't done anything, apparently, except hide his phone. And take off his shirt. All in the name of love.

Time to show Debbie what a chill and relaxed guy he was.

Bob shrugged one shoulder. "I didn't do it," he said in a voice that he hoped conveyed how little he cared. But inside, he was kind of freaking out. "I guess we'll find out when we get there."

Debbie stared at him as the elevator chimed and the doors opened. She stayed rooted in place, and only stepped out after Bob and Sandy had left her there.

Bob added a swagger to his steps as he walked out of the hotel and toward the car, pretending he didn't know if Debbie was behind him or not. In reality, he knew exactly how far she was behind him, and he adjusted his pace accordingly.

Man, this was exhausting. But Debbie was worth it. And he'd do anything to prove that he was who she was meant to be with.

Chapter Eleven

D ebbie watched Bob interact with a couple of students who had stopped at their table. She had been about to introduce herself, but he had stepped in and asked them about their interests and if they had ever traveled through Amor before. It was like a stranger had replaced Bob. He was animated and interested in the lives of the people he talked to. And when he, Debbie, and Sandy had arrived late and their spot had been given to a last-minute arrival, he hadn't freaked out. He had simply asked where a good place for them to set up would be.

And then there was the fact that he'd slept in because he hadn't been able to find his phone that morning. If she hadn't seen it for herself, she'd never have believed it. Not only had he slept in, but he had answered the door half-dressed. Oh gosh, when she had seen him without a shirt—her heart had literally stopped. She couldn't breathe. Did he work out? She'd never seen him so much as speed-walk, but no one got abs like that without doing something.

Debbie sat down in a seat next to Sandy, who had been playing on her phone. She quickly shoved it into her pocket, like there was something she didn't want Debbie to see.

"Bored?" Debbie asked.

Sandy blushed, though she had no reason to, and gave a noncommittal shrug. "I thought you'd have me running around doing stuff for you, but it looks like it's a one-man show today."

"Yeah, it does." Debbie paused, then asked, "Is Bob acting weird today, or is it just me?"

"You mean, weirder than normal?"

Debbie laughed. "Yeah."

"He's not freaking out about everything, so that's been nice," Sandy said. "Maybe he just needed to get away from the office."

"Yeah, maybe." But Debbie wasn't sure that was it.

The two students walked away with pamphlets and Bob walked over to Debbie and Sandy, grinning. "So, how am I doing?"

"You're a pro," Sandy said. "They should make this your permanent position."

Bob's smile slipped and Debbie swore she saw panic flit across his features. He quickly recovered, though, and grinned. "Maybe you should put in a good word to the mayor for me."

"Happy to," Sandy said. Her phone buzzed and she pulled it out. When she glanced at the screen she laughed softly, but then realized that Debbie was watching her. "Funny cat meme," Sandy said before stuffing the phone back into her pocket.

Okay, something weird was going on. Bob and Sandy weren't what Debbie would define as normal, but they were acting strange, even for them. She was going to demand that they both tell her what was going on, but a group of students walked up at that moment and Bob hurried away to greet them.

"I feel completely useless," Debbie muttered. "Anytime I try to talk to someone, Bob jumps in and takes over."

"You're complaining that you are being paid to not work?" Sandy asked.

True, it sounded silly when Sandy put it that way. But Debbie had been asked to come along for a reason. Bob was supposed to take care of logistics, and she would use her expertise as a business owner to share the opportunities that Amor held. And even though all the students left their table with a smile and a pamphlet in hand, she noticed that none of them had written down their information to be contacted directly about employment opportunities.

"I need to go for a walk," Debbie said, standing up.

"Okay," Sandy said, pulling her phone out again. She didn't ask where Debbie was going or when she'd be back.

With a final glance back toward Bob, Debbie left and made her way across campus. The buildings all looked the same as the other university they had visited. The landscape was perfectly manicured and everything was in order. But it didn't have character, and there was nothing that made it unique except an onslaught of school colors that differed slightly from the last university they had visited.

It was like Bob. Orderly and predictable. But unlike this university, his predictability was what made Bob different. He was someone she could rely on, who kept her grounded. He was the yin to her yang. She hadn't realized how much she appreciated that about him until today—when he wasn't any of the things that she needed.

Debbie didn't know how long she had been walking around campus, but when she returned to the student union building, she found Bob pacing in front of the table, looking frazzled. "Everything okay?" she asked as she approached him.

"Where were you?" he demanded, running a hand through his hair.

"Out for a walk," Debbie said, unsure why he was so upset. He had obviously had everything under control when she'd left.

"You've been gone for an hour. I turned around and you'd disappeared." He released a long breath.

"You could have called."

"Yes, if I had a spare second," Bob said. "But there were swarms of bright-eyed young people...*swarms*. And you were nowhere to be seen."

"You were busy, so I told Sandy where I was going," Debbie said, pointing back to where Sandy had sat. Except it was now an empty chair.

Bob's lips formed a tight line. "She's been gone for the past hour as well."

"She must have got restless," Debbie said with a small shrug.

Bob balked. "How? We've been on our feet for the past four hours, talking to a steady stream of students."

"No, that's what *you've* been doing. Sandy and I were over there trying to stay awake," Debbie said, nodding to the two empty chairs. "We could have taken turns talking to students like we did at the other university; that way, you wouldn't have to be on your feet all afternoon." Her gaze scanned the table. "You're out of pamphlets. Sandy wanted to be useful and she could have gone to the car to get more for you. But you didn't want anyone's help, so when it was obvious that her services weren't needed, she probably wandered off to find the library."

Bob slumped into one of the chairs. "Everything was manageable at first, so I thought I could do it on my own. But then you guys left and a rush of students came. I couldn't give them the attention they needed, so I just shoved pamphlets at them all."

"Why?" Debbie asked, sitting next to him. "We are supposed to be a team. But anytime one of us tried to help, you immediately took over."

Bob muttered something, but his words were too soft to be discernible.

"You're going to have to repeat that."

He threw her an anxious glance, then said, "I wanted you to think of me as capable."

Debbie stared. "Why would I think otherwise? You're the reason anything gets done in Town Hall. You keep that place running. And you're the reason things have gone so smoothly on this trip."

"Until today."

"Yes, until today," Debbie said. "But why would you think you are anything less than capable?"

Bob rubbed a hand over the stubble on his jaw. "I don't—not really. Not when it comes to doing my job. I know I'm good at what I do. But not in the ways that really count."

He looked so distraught that Debbie couldn't help but place a hand on his knee, hoping it would give him a little comfort. "And what would those be?"

Bob looked at her hand, then, with slight hesitation, rested his own on top. "Everything you needed from me—before—but I couldn't deliver."

Debbie's breath hitched. "I'm so sorry if I ever treated you like you weren't enough," she said.

Was it possible that it hadn't been him who had driven the wedge between them, but it had actually been her fault?

"It doesn't matter," Bob said, standing up. "I tried to be someone different today—the person you deserve. I purposely turned my alarm off and I tried to be spontaneous and do things on the fly. But that's not who I am. It's time I stopped holding on to a mirage."

Debbie leaped to her feet. "Today...you were acting like that...for me?"

All this time she had been acting the part of the victim, but suddenly it felt like she was the one who needed to make amends and ask for Bob's forgiveness. How had she not seen it before?

"I like the original version of you much better," she said.

"Really?" Bob looked shocked by this news.

She played with the hem of her shirt until she mustered up the courage to nod and say, "Maybe, if you went back to being you, we could give us another try?"

Her words seemed to shock both of them, but it felt right. If their failed relationship had been Debbie's fault, didn't she owe it to Bob to try again, and be the person he deserved? What if being placed on this trip together had been divine intervention—a second chance for them? And if it ended in disaster, well, they wouldn't be any worse off than they had been.

Bob dropped his gaze, and Debbie was afraid he'd say no. Maybe they had too much baggage to try to make this work. She wouldn't blame him for thinking so.

"Okay." He looked up and gave her a soft smile.

Debbie's heart stuttered. "Okay." She wasn't sure what else to say, or what this all meant. Were they dating again?

"So..." Bob seemed to be having the same problem.

Debbie looked around and saw that the ballroom where they were situated was starting to empty out. "It looks like they are done for the day," she said lamely. "Guess that means we should pack up. And find Sandy."

"Sorry, I'm here," Sandy said, rushing up.

"Find any good books?" Debbie asked, thankful for the distraction.

Sandy tilted her head to one side. "Books?"

"I figured you'd gone to check out the library."

Sandy's face reddened as she stuttered, "Oh-oh, yeah. Um...I mean, I didn't go to the library. Just a walk. Like you."

All Debbie could think of to say was, "Uh-huh." She couldn't keep the disbelief out of her tone, and the red in Sandy's cheeks deepened. Debbie didn't want to embarrass Sandy, especially in front of Bob. Whatever was going on with her, it could wait. "Want to help me pack everything back up in these boxes?"

Sandy released a long breath and looked relieved that Debbie wasn't going to ask any more questions. "Yeah, of course."

It didn't take more than a couple of minutes to throw everything in, and Debbie couldn't help but feel a little disappointed that they only had one more career fair to visit. After tomorrow, the ride home would be all that was left.

Chapter Twelve

T he next day sped by quickly, and with the last career fair completed, an emptiness permeated the air.

The next morning, Bob packed up his suitcase slowly. Not that it would have taken very long anyway, considering this had been the third city they'd been to in almost as many days, and most of his stuff had never made it out of the suitcase this time around.

But leaving this time felt different. And even though he and Debbie had decided a couple of days before that they were going to try the dating thing again, nothing had come of it. It had almost made things more awkward between them than before. They only talked about safe subjects, always skirting the issue. Of course, it could have been because Sandy was usually with them, but Bob didn't think that was it.

There had been once or twice when he and Debbie had been alone and he had reached for her hand, but she had conveniently needed to tuck a strand of hair behind her ear at the same moment, or use the restroom. She had been the one to suggest that they try again, so he couldn't figure out what the problem was. But anytime he tried asking, he found they were suddenly talking about something completely random, like the endangerment of pandas, having no idea how they got on the subject in the first place. Pandas, it turned out, weren't endangered anymore, only vulnerable, thank goodness.

But once they returned to Amor, Bob was afraid it would only get worse, and more awkward. And that whatever they had started to rekindle on this trip would be smothered.

He glanced at his watch. It was only seven o'clock in the morning, but there was a chance that the women would already be up. He felt weird about knocking on their door, but maybe Debbie would respond to a text.

Heading down to breakfast. Want to join me?

Bob triple-checked under the bed and in the crevices of the room to make sure he didn't leave anything while he waited for her response. But she didn't answer, and there were only so many drawers and corners he could check.

He turned his phone off and then on again to reset it, just in case, but it still showed zero texts. With a grunt of frustration, he threw the phone on the bed next to his suitcase and headed to the elevator. When the bell chimed and the doors opened, he moved to step inside, but was surprised to see Debbie already there.

She looked equally surprised and didn't seem to know whether she was getting off or not.

"I texted you," Bob finally said, placing his foot in the path of the elevator door so it wouldn't shut.

"I know," Debbie said. "Sorry, I couldn't sleep and went down to breakfast early."

Bob tilted his head. "You could have responded and told me that."

"I should have. Sorry," she said, dropping her gaze.

There was an awkward pause between them, then they both spoke at once.

"Do you not want to give me a chance?" Bob asked as Debbie said, "I don't know how to do this."

It took a moment for her words to register, and then his heart crumbled. "You don't know how, or you don't want to?"

"I want to," Debbie said in earnest, her gaze snapping back to him. He could see that she meant it, but sometimes wanting wasn't enough. "I just don't know how. Starting over from scratch is much easier than retrying something that has already..." Her voice trailed off.

"Failed," Bob said, finishing her sentence.

Debbie hesitated, but then nodded. "Yeah."

"Is that why you've been distancing yourself?"

Her shoulders slumped. "I haven't meant to, but it appears that I'm not very good at relationships. I'm pretty sure it was me who messed things up the first time, and now I'm back at it again. I just don't know how I'm supposed to act."

Someone cleared their throat from behind Bob, and he turned to see a young family waiting behind him, their luggage in tow.

"Sorry," he mumbled, moving aside. Debbie scurried out of the elevator after him, but he waited until the family was gone before he turned to her. With just a slight hesitation, he took her hand in his and said, "Your fault? Our relationship ended because of me. It's always been me."

Debbie dropped his hand. "I know that's what I said, but I'm not so sure anymore. I was blind to who you are and what you needed from me. I was selfish, and I think I have a lot of making up to do." She paused and shook her head. "But it will never be like when we met for the first time. There isn't a natural progression, or an order to how it's supposed to go, you know?"

Bob's heart thundered in his chest. He couldn't let Debbie walk away, not this time. "I know. I get it. It's weird. But couldn't we pretend it was the first time?"

Debbie cocked a skeptical eyebrow. "You mean, act like we haven't dated before?"

Bob nodded quickly, feeling more excited about the prospect. "Yes. We shove memories aside and start over." He stepped away from Debbie. "Here, I'll start."

He walked down the hallway a bit, then returned, walking like he didn't have a care in the world. Bob paused at the elevator doors, then glanced at Debbie. "I'm sorry, were you waiting to go down? How rude of me to just cut in front of you like that."

Debbie's lip quirked up. "I was just deciding if I wanted to go down for a second breakfast or not, but hadn't made up my mind yet."

Bob took a step toward her. "I know I'm being forward, but if you wanted to join me, I wouldn't say no." He stuck out his hand toward her. "I'm Bobby, by the way."

A little gasp of surprise escaped Debbie's lips. He'd never given himself a nickname before, but it seemed appropriate for the situation. "I'm Deb," she said, taking his hand and shaking it. "It's a pleasure to meet you."

"It's all mine." Bob raised her hand to his lips and kissed it gently.

Debbie fanned herself with her free hand. "I can tell I'll need to be careful around you. You're a charmer."

A burst of happiness exploded within Bob and he grinned. He knew he was just pretending to be the dashing bachelor, but maybe there was a part of Bobby lying dormant inside him that he could awaken from time to time. Because, honestly, Bob didn't feel like he was being someone he wasn't. It was more like he was allowing himself to be someone he normally kept in check.

"Does that mean you'll join me?" Bob asked.

"I'd be delighted."

Bob pressed the down button on the elevator and felt lighter than he had in years.

BY NINE O'CLOCK, THEIR luggage was in the back of the car and they were ready to head home. Debbie didn't offer her front seat to Sandy this time, and instead smiled at Bob as he put the key in the ignition.

"It's very kind of you to offer me a ride home," she said, continuing to pretend that this was their first time meeting.

"I couldn't very well leave you stranded, now could I?" he asked. "I still can't believe we're from the same town and have never run into each other."

Sandy sat forward and looked between the two like they had gone crazy, which was understandable. She handed one of her therapist's business cards to Bob. "Have you ever considered couples therapy?"

Bob laughed and sent a quick wink in Debbie's direction. It sent a thrill up his spine when her cheeks reddened and she returned his smile.

"Shall we go, *Bobby*?" she asked, emphasizing the name of his new persona while putting on a pair of sunglasses and tilting her seat back.

"We shall." He turned the key, but instead of starting, the car sputtered, then sat quiet. Dread replaced the exhilaration he'd felt just seconds before. He tried again but received the same result.

"Please tell me that was you just messing around," Sandy said, her obvious anxiety mirroring Bob's.

"I don't mess around, especially about stuff like this," Bob said. He hated that his tone had reverted to his usual businesslike manner, and how easily his personality overpowered any hold that 'Bobby' had had on him.

"Well, where I come from, we have a quick fix for this type of thing," Debbie said. Her smile was more forced than it had been, but she slid her sunglasses up on top of her head and he saw that her eyes still shone bright. She jumped out of the car and slammed her door shut.

"What is she doing?" Bob muttered. His breath caught in his throat as Debbie started banging on the front of the car in a rhythm that seemed awfully familiar. He debated telling her that she was going to dent his car, but he couldn't bring himself to do it; she looked like she was having so much fun, and he loved seeing her happy.

Debbie finished her drum solo by sliding across the car on her butt, then opening the passenger door and jumping back into her seat.

He stared, open-mouthed. "Did you just do the drum solo from the song 'Wipe Out'?"

Her beautiful, genuine smile returned. "You're just full of surprises today. I didn't think you'd recognize it."

Bob felt a surge of pride at having some pop culture knowledge, and being able to show it off for Debbie. "Yes, well, let's see if the car recognized it." He stroked the steering wheel a couple of times, then turned the key. The car sputtered a few times, but just when it sounded like it would die again, it rumbled to life. "Yes!" Bob yelled, slamming his hands against the steering wheel. The car gave a whine, and he immediately apologized.

"It looks like your car has good taste in music," Debbie said.

He looked her in the eyes—man, he had to try hard not to get lost in them. "Thank you," he said quietly.

She gave him a shy smile. "Happy to help."

"I have a feeling I'm going to enjoy getting to know you, Deb," Bob said, taking his own sunglasses off the car visor and slipping them on.

"There's a lot to learn," she said.

"Seriously, what is up with you two?" Sandy asked from the back seat.

"It's just a beautiful day is all," Bob said as he laughed and shifted the car into drive. He checked the gas gauge. "I'm going to try to make it to Amor without stopping. I don't want to risk the car not being able to start again." The thought was a little disappointing, as he'd hoped to drag the trip out a little bit, but it was better than not making it back at all.

"What if I have to use the bathroom?" Sandy asked.

"We can probably keep the car running while we take turns at the rest area," Bob said, pulling out of the parking lot.

As he merged onto the freeway, Debbie stretched out a bit before her hand found a resting spot on his leg, her fingers drumming on his thigh. His heart rate accelerated and he found himself struggling to focus on the road.

Debbie must have noticed, because she asked, "Is this all right?" She waved her fingers at him. "There isn't a lot of room and I was trying to get comfortable."

Bob swallowed hard but couldn't keep from smiling. If the only way she could get comfortable was by touching him, he was okay with that. "Sure," he said, as if not caring one way or the other. "Whatever you need."

"Did you buy any more of those ranch chips?" Sandy asked, reminding Bob that he and Debbie weren't alone. "That would make me comfortable." She snorted back laughter.

Bob's natural reaction was to pull away from Debbie, but he stopped himself. He would need to get used to people seeing them together, so he might as well start now. Because no matter what Debbie said, he knew that his aversion to public affection had been a major reason for their break-up.

And when he forced himself to relax and laugh with Sandy, Bob realized that going on this trip had been the best thing that could have ever happened to him. He could honestly say that he was happier than he had been in years; he'd have to thank Mayor McAllister when they got back.

Scratch that.

The mayor could never know. It would only encourage her.

Chapter Thirteen

Debbie squinted, attempting to see anything that might indicate they were still driving on the road. Wind whipped around the car as they slowly moved forward, but the dust had reduced the visibility to almost nothing.

"Maybe we should pull over," she said.

"Pull over where?" Bob asked, running a hand through his hair. "I might drive right into a ravine for all I know."

"But we've passed a zillion huge electronic signs that said, 'If you're caught in a dust storm, pull over, keep your seatbelts on, turn off your lights and take your feet off the brakes.' I doubt we are going to fly off a cliff when they are telling us to pull over and wait it out."

"But if we keep going, even if it's slowly, we'll at least be making progress. What if the storm lasts for hours?"

Debbie could hear the stress in his voice. The car shook with each gust, and she could understand wanting to get through the storm as quickly as possible. But their visibility was so low that—

"Brake!" she screeched.

Bob slammed on the brakes and the car screeched to a halt. They had stopped less than a foot from a large semi-truck that they hadn't seen in front of them.

Debbie's heart raced as she realized how close they had been to smashing into it.

"There has to be a better way," Sandy said in a quivering voice.

"Well, the first step is to figure out where we are," Debbie said. "The truck is stopped and their brake lights aren't on. That might mean we were actually driving along the edge of the road."

Bob's hands held tight to the steering wheel. "I guess I'm forced to follow the rules, then."

"I didn't know you were such a rebel," Debbie teased. "I kind of like it, though."

He unclenched his hands from the steering wheel and shot her a look she couldn't quite distinguish as he shifted the car into park, turned off the lights, and then moved his foot from the brake. "See, I knew it. You've always wanted to date the rule breaker, you just didn't want to admit it."

"I was kidding," she said, throwing her hands up in exasperation. "Can't a girl flirt anymore?"

Bob opened his mouth to answer, but Sandy beat him to the punch.

"Why are you flirting with Bob?" she asked.

Sheesh. Debbie liked Sandy and everything, but this was turning into a third wheel kind of thing. It must have been super awkward for Sandy, but Debbie supposed it was good for Bob to practice not hiding his relationships from other people.

When Debbie glanced back but didn't answer right away, realization spread across Sandy's face. "Is that why you two have been acting so weird?" she asked in a low voice. "Is something happening between you two?" She grinned and seemed excited by the prospect.

Debbie shared a look with Bob, and she waited for him to respond. This would be a test to see if he was capable of having a relationship in public.

Bob didn't say anything for so long that Debbie had given up hope and was about to respond that there most certainly wasn't anything going on between them, but then Bob straightened up and said, "Yes. We still have feelings for each other and we'd like to try to date again. We even kissed passionately at the animal rehabilitation center, and I'd say that things are looking very optimistic."

Both Debbie and Sandy stared at Bob. That was a bit more information than Debbie would have shared, but she had to give him credit where credit was due.

Sandy burst into giggles again. She was like a teenage girl who was discovering romantic relationships for the first time. "David said your hair was messed up more than it should have been," she said to Debbie. "He looked at me like I should have known what that meant." She paused, her eyes bright. "I do now!" She burst into another round of laughter.

Debbie groaned and felt her ears heating with embarrassment, but she still couldn't help but smile.

That was when the car jerked, accompanied by a loud crash.

Debbie lurched forward, but luckily she had kept her seatbelt on and it kept her from flying out of her seat. A shocked silence settled in the car. "Sandy, are you okay?" she asked, turning back.

"Ughh." A pause. "Yeah, I think so. I hit my knee and arm on the door, so I'll probably have some bruises."

Bob seemed to be in shock, staring ahead.

"You okay?" Debbie asked, shaking his shoulder.

He blinked a few times before finally turning to her. "Yeah." He didn't sound fine, though.

"I think we should get both of you checked out at the nearest hospital," Debbie said.

That seemed to bring Bob back and he shook his head. "No, really, I'm fine."

"Okay," she said, still uncertain, but there wasn't much she could do about it right then.

Debbie unbuckled her seatbelt so she could turn and get a better idea of what, or who, had hit them.

"Sit back down," Bob said. "What if something else hits us?" An edge of panic laced his voice.

"What if there's someone who needs our help?" she asked, straining, but failing, to see beyond the dust that covered the back window. "Turn on the windshield wipers so I can see better." When they didn't turn on, she slid back into her seat. "Fine, I'll do it."

"I'm trying," Bob said, turning the dials. He looked up. "I think it's dead."

"Did someone say dead?" Sandy screeched from the back seat. "It's the person that hit us, isn't it? We have been involved in a fatal car crash and now I have another thing to be haunted by for the next decade."

"Sandy," Debbie barked, not bothering to keep her voice down. The stress and the noise and keeping everyone calm was too much, and she was nearing her breaking point. "No one is dead. Well, the car might be. But no people."

Sandy's mouth formed an O. "It's hard to hear back here with the wind and everything," she said apologetically, her gaze now on her hands. They were folded in her lap, like when a child felt shame for doing something wrong.

It tugged on Debbie's heartstrings. "I'm sorry," she said. "I shouldn't have yelled at you."

"You were right to. I was freaking out without understanding what was going on."

"No, there is no excuse."

Debbie avoided Bob's gaze, not liking that he had witnessed her burst of emotion. She wanted him to think highly of her, and she wondered what he thought of her losing her temper.

"So...just to be clear," Sandy started, her words coming out slowly and haltingly, "you said that the car is dead."

"Yes," Debbie said.

"Does this worry either of you?" Sandy asked, even slower still.

Yeah, it did. But telling Sandy that would only make matters worse. Besides, while the storm raged on, they couldn't go anywhere. "We'll figure it out once we know where we are," Debbie said.

"Okay," Sandy said, obviously not convinced.

Bob caught Debbie's gaze, and his eyes seemed to be asking a question, but she couldn't figure out what they were saying. After a moment, he released a sigh and looked away.

The trip home that had started out so well seemed to be falling apart, and Debbie didn't know how to stop it.

Chapter Fourteen

Bob had never been so happy to see the sun as he had when the dust settled and they could see again. He cautiously opened his door, not sure what to expect. Dust blanketed the earth, but he could tell that they were indeed on the side of the road, and there weren't any ravines or cliffs that they had been in danger of driving over. At least Debbie had been right about that.

Bob wandered a little further away from the road, needing some time to himself. As soon as the storm had passed Debbie had jumped into action, calling the police about the accident and the tow truck to help get them to a repair shop. But he couldn't handle all that—not yet. He was too immersed in his own self-loathing, and no matter what he tried, he couldn't shake it. When they had been hit from behind, and he now saw that it had been a pickup truck, he had frozen. He hadn't gone into fight or flight mode—he'd gone into fright mode. The kind that makes deer stand in the middle of a street, staring at the headlights of a vehicle that would soon run them over.

When Debbie had brought him back to his senses, he'd realized that he didn't deserve someone like her. He wasn't Bobby, his alter ego. He was Bob, who was scared and anxious all the time. Though he hadn't been able to admit it to Sandy, Bob was no stranger to a therapist's office, and he'd heard every trick in the book. The one that was the worst was positive affirmations—ugh. They only made him feel worse, because he didn't believe a word he was saying.

Debbie deserved someone better. He knew this, so why was he pretending otherwise?

Bob realized he'd wandered further into the desert than he had intended. When he turned to walk back, Debbie was standing next to him. "I didn't hear you," he said.

"I know. Those must be some pretty heavy thoughts you're lugging around." She didn't look at him with disgust, which made him feel worse about it all.

"Never mind my thoughts. Let's get the car taken care of," he said, brushing past her.

She reached out and took his hand. "It will be an hour before the tow truck can get out here, and I've already exchanged information with the driver of the truck that hit us. Why don't we just go on a walk for a bit?"

He stared at their entwined hands. "What about Sandy?"

"She's reading a book in the back seat and devouring a bag of ranch chips she found under the seat. She'll be fine."

Bob couldn't think of any other excuses, so he nodded, and they picked their way through the cactus. He kept an eye out for rattlesnakes and scorpions, not wanting to add venom to the list of awful things the day had brought with it.

Debbie spoke first. "I know I wasn't kind with Sandy during the storm and I already apologized to her, but I feel that I should apologize to you too."

That made Bob stop. "What?" He wondered if he looked as bewildered as he felt. "You helped her calm down. She wouldn't have even heard you above the wind if you hadn't raised your voice. That's why she was having a panic attack in the first place—because she misheard you."

Debbie turned so they were facing each other. "You aren't disappointed in me?" She sounded so hopeful that Bob couldn't help but laugh and pull her in.

"Never," he said, then stepped back, but kept his hands on her hips. "Your hair tickles, by the way."

"Sorry," she said, then paused. "Actually, not sorry. Hair was meant to be ticklish, so I take that one back."

Bob's love for this incredible woman grew by the minute, and his gaze flickered to her lips. He wondered what she'd do if he kissed her again, right there in the desert. But then he remembered why he was out there in the first place, and dread settled in his stomach. He stepped away. "We should be getting back. The cops should be here soon, right?"

Debbie's smile faded, and her brows furrowed. "What's wrong?"

Bob thought about spilling his heart to her, but admitting to himself that he was a coward was very different from having to say it out loud. Especially when it would be to someone he loved—and someone he wanted to love him back.

"You have to start trusting me sometime," she said softly.

He stared past her into the wilderness. "If I say what is on my mind, I could lose you. Again."

"If you don't, it may have the same result."

Bob's gaze snapped back to her. She didn't seem like she was trying to be vengeful, but the words still hurt.

Debbie gave a slight shake of her head. "I know you like your privacy, but this trip has opened my eyes to how little I actually knew about you when we were dating. How was our relationship ever going to work when you were just as much as stranger to me when we broke up as when we first met? And vice versa. I don't want to pressure you to do what makes you feel uncomfortable, but discomfort is part of growing and becoming stronger. And I think we both have room for growth."

She stared at him, like she was challenging him to walk away.

But Debbie had made a good argument, and he knew she was right. About everything. And he supposed that if the relationship wasn't going to work out, if she couldn't handle the real him, then now was the time to find out, instead of another two years down the road.

Bob sucked in a long breath. "You need someone who is your equal," he started, picking his words carefully. "But I don't believe that someone is me." Whoa. He hadn't meant to say that last part.

Debbie's eyes narrowed. "Are you breaking up with me? Again? We haven't even made it forty-eight hours yet."

"No," Bob said quickly. "But I'm giving you an out."

Her features relaxed, though she now seemed more perplexed than anything. "Why on earth would I want that?"

"You saw me earlier." He could hardly stand the disgust he felt for himself. "We were rear-ended and I completely crumbled. That's not someone you want to be with. You need someone who will conquer the world with you, not hide under a rock waiting for everything to be okay again."

Debbie laughed, and annoyance bubbled up. This was something incredibly personal to him, and she was making light of it.

"I'm sorry," she said, "but with the way you were acting, I thought it was more serious than that."

"I *am* serious."

She sobered, but her eyes were still laughing at him. "I know, but the thing is, everyone responds differently to those situations, and it's something outside of our control. It doesn't change how I feel about you. Truthfully, it didn't even faze me."

If it didn't matter, why was it still bothering him so much? She'd said it was inconsequential to their relationship, but she couldn't really mean that. Didn't she want someone who was ready to stand strong, no matter the obstacles they faced?

"I can see that you don't believe me," Debbie said. She held out a hand to Bob. He hesitated, but then placed his hand in hers. She pulled him forward toward her. "What would it take to prove it to you?"

Bob didn't know if there was anything, so long as he didn't believe it himself. It was those awful positive affirmations all over again. He was still thinking it over, trying to come up with something, when her lips landed on his. At first he was so surprised that he forgot to kiss back. But as Debbie wrapped her arms around his waist and tightened her grip, he jumped into the action, his lips cupping hers. He placed a hand behind her neck, deepening their hungry kisses, but Debbie lost her balance and tipped backward.

He tightened his grip around her, keeping her from hitting the ground, and he held her in a dip, their eyes locked on one another.

"See?" she said. "You're strong enough to catch me when I fall. I never doubted it for a minute."

Bob eased Debbie back up. "Thank you," he said.

"I didn't do anything," she said, though her grin suggested otherwise.

"Are you two going to make out again, or can we start processing your collision?" a voice called from the direction of the car.

They both looked up at the same time. A police officer stood next to the road. Sandy was with him and they were both grinning.

"And you always wondered why I liked our privacy when we were dating," Bob muttered. Sandy was one thing, but an officer of the law was now mocking them?

"Yeah, I kind of get it now," Debbie said as they stepped around a large cactus, her own cheeks flushed. "But that doesn't mean we can hide forever."

Bob knew that. At least a part of him did. But another, louder, part of him still insisted that it was better to establish a strong relationship before letting anyone else in on things.

It didn't take long for the officer to fill out his police report, and it wasn't much longer before the tow truck arrived.

"What's the closest town?" Bob asked, wondering how long repairs would take. They must still be at least four hours away from Amor.

"Carlsbad," the officer said. "It's about thirty miles from here. They only got one garage there, though, so it might take them a little bit to get to it."

"As in Carlsbad Caverns?" Sandy asked, perking up.

"Yeah. Since it'll probably take at least a day or two, I would recommend taking in the sights while you're there."

Sandy spun toward Bob and asked, "Today is Saturday, right?"

"Yeah."

"Can we go to the bat flight tonight? And then the caves tomorrow?" Her eyes pleaded with him, and he knew he couldn't say no. Not that he would have wanted to anyway. He loved bats. They were one of the most misunderstood and interesting mammals.

"Sure," he said. "So long as we can find transportation."

"The garage will set you up with a loaner, if they have one available," the officer said, handing Bob a strip of paper with the information he'd need for the insurance company. "You'll want to get a move on. They close in an hour."

The tow truck driver already had the vehicle in position, and it wasn't another fifteen minutes before they were all crammed in the cab of his truck. He wasn't thrilled when Bob insisted they all ride together, but Debbie was able to talk the driver into letting the three of them squeeze into a seat only meant for one person.

When they arrived at the garage, they tumbled out of the cab, and Debbie was grateful it had only been thirty miles. She was pretty sure she had an imprint from the door's handle in her side.

They wandered into a small office, where a man with a long red mustache sat at a computer. He glanced up at them as they filed in, then returned to what he had been doing.

"Jeff told me you guys would be in," he said.

Bob tilted his head to one side. "Jeff?"

"Yeah, the officer that helped you guys out with your collision. That was some sandstorm, but not surprising, considering it's that time of the year."

"Right."

There was a long pause. The clicks of the man's keyboard and the whirring of a tool from the garage were the only sounds that broke the silence.

"So..." Debbie started. "When will you be able to take a look at the car?"

The man didn't respond right away. He continued typing for another moment, then finally pressed 'enter' and pushed away from his desk. "Right now." He held out his hand to Bob, who looked at it, then realized that the man was asking for his keys.

They followed him outside where he attempted to start the car. It did the same thing it had at the hotel, trying to start, but failing.

"Did the car accelerate?" the man asked. "Like going up hills or when you were passing others."

Debbie stifled a laugh. She'd bet that Bob had never passed another car in his life.

"Going up hills was a bit tough," he answered. "It was like I had to get a running start to get over them."

"And what about the rpm gauge?"

"It sat at zero for most of the trip."

Debbie turned and stared. "You didn't tell me that. I thought everything was going well until the accident."

"I didn't want to worry you or Sandy," he said.

Except, that was a huge deal. If something was wrong, Bob couldn't help but panic and talk out loud as he attempted to figure the problem out. He'd probably realized that Sandy would freak out, and he'd saved her from that.

"Thank you," she said. "That was really thoughtful of you."

Bob's cheeks turned pink and he turned back to the man. "So, do you have any ideas?"

"Oh yeah, and you're not going to like it. I need to have a closer look at the car, of course, but I'd bet anything you need a new fuel pump. Probably a new hose too."

"Why wouldn't I like that?"

The man grimaced. "Because it's going to cost you close to a thousand dollars."

Bob's pink cheeks were suddenly devoid of color, and for a brief second he placed a hand on the wall, as if he needed it to help keep him upright. He quickly straightened, though, and said in a matter-of-fact voice, "And how long will that take to repair?"

"I won't be able to get the parts until Monday, so you can plan on being able to head out on Tuesday."

"But that's three days from now," Bob yelped.

The man shrugged. "We're not open on Sundays. Gotta take a day off sometime, ya know?"

"How about you take next Wednesday off instead," Bob suggested, his tone hopeful.

The man shook his head. "Sorry, but it's going to be ready Tuesday. Good news is that someone just dropped off one of our loaner cars about ten minutes ago; otherwise, I wouldn't have had anything for you."

Bob turned his back and muttered to Debbie, "Let's drive the loaner car to Amor, and then we can drive back on Tuesday."

She was going to protest, but the mechanic spoke up first.

"I can hear you, and that car doesn't leave Carlsbad."

Bob released a long sigh. "Fine. And thank you."

"Why are you in such a hurry to leave?" Debbie asked as the man left to get the keys for the loaner car. "We get to enjoy a little downtime after working all week. Together."

The corner of Bob's lips twitched up, and he suddenly didn't seem to mind the idea of staying. "I suppose you're right. I was concerned about not being at work on Monday, but Daniel can handle an extra couple of days without me. And I do need to learn how to relax."

"That's the spirit," Debbie said. She turned to ask Sandy if she wanted to call her mother to break the news, or if Zoe should. Except, Debbie stopped when she realized that Sandy didn't have a clue what was going on around her. She was staring at her phone, her fingers flying over the screen and a grin spread so wide across her face that Debbie didn't think anyone had ever had a reason to be as happy as Sandy was in that moment. "What's up?" she asked, touching the woman lightly on her shoulder.

Sandy didn't acknowledge Debbie's presence until she had finished sending her message, then she looked up, the smile not diminishing. "I have a dinner date."

Chapter Fifteen

Bob spun toward Sandy. Debbie looked as shocked as he felt. "I'm sorry, did you say you have a dinner date?"

Sandy nodded, still grinning. "Technically it will be linner. You know, lunch mixed with dinner, since it's not that late yet."

"B-but how? The only person we've met here is the mechanic." Bob's stomach dropped. "Did he ask you out?" There was no way he was letting Sandy go to dinner with a man they had known for five minutes.

But to his relief, Sandy's eyes widened and she looked horrified. "Oh my gosh, no. My date is actually on his way here to pick me up."

"What, now?" Bob peered out the office window, but didn't see any cars pulling in.

"How exactly did you meet this man?" Debbie asked slowly. "I noticed you've been on your phone a lot. Was it through Tinder or a dating app like that?"

Oh, that was so much worse than the scenarios he'd come up with.

Sandy's horror intensified. "Really? You think I just picked up a Tinder date in the few minutes we've been in town?"

"Do you even know what Tinder is?" Bob asked Sandy. He barely understood the dating app, and he wasn't the one who'd been homebound for the past fifteen years.

"Uh, I do know how to use the Internet," she said, her frown giving way to an amused smile. "I know that I don't always give the best first impression, but I'm not as naive as most people think."

"Anyway," Debbie said, "back to the topic at hand." She lowered her voice to a conspiratorial whisper. "Who's the lucky guy?" It seemed that she was no longer worried, and instead excited about meeting this mysterious date.

"Wait, we're actually letting her do this?" Bob asked, not wanting to know how many ways Rebecca could kill him if anything happened to her daughter. He'd seen the equipment in her bakery—she was dangerous.

"She's not a child," Debbie said, giving him a pointed look. "She's old enough to make her own choices."

"All I'm saying is we need to meet the guy. And approve of him. And get his social security number so we can do a background check."

Sandy laughed. "Yeah, right."

Bob stared at her, stone-faced. "I can call Daniel and have him run the name faster than it would take you to jump on the back of your date's Harley."

Her smile slipped and her voice came out in a hoarse whisper. "You'd do that?"

"Of course he wouldn't," Debbie said, throwing a glance his way. "Because we trust you."

Bob returned her look. "Can I talk to you for a moment?"

Since when had they become squabbling parents? And to an adult that neither of them was related to?

Debbie gave Sandy what looked like a reassuring pat on the arm, then followed Bob outside the office.

"What's wrong with you?" Bob whispered, though no one else was there to hear the conversation. "You seriously are okay with her running off with some random guy?"

"Of course I'm not," Debbie said, matching his whisper. "The second he arrives, you need to get both his first and last name, preferably off his driver's license, so we know he's not lying. And then as soon as they leave, you call Daniel about that background check."

Bob felt like he had just gotten off the Tilt-A-Whirl and everything was still spinning. "If you agree with me, why did you say all that stuff in there?"

"Because we don't want her to think we're checking up on him. She needs to feel completely secure, or else she'll tip him off."

Debbie had never been more attractive than at that moment. He pulled her in and planted a long kiss on her lips.

"What was that for?" she asked, smiling.

"Because every day on this trip I've been able to get a glimpse of the little things that make you the amazing person you are," he said, sneaking another little kiss on her forehead.

The sound of a car pulling into the parking lot made Bob step back. His gaze landed on a black sedan. "Get the license plate number," he mumbled to Debbie as he walked out to meet the driver of the car that had just stopped in front of them.

Sandy rushed out of the office at that moment. "Whatever you're thinking of doing, don't," she told Bob.

The driver's side door opened, and out stepped a man. He seemed awfully familiar.

"David?" Debbie said, moving past Bob.

He hadn't recognized David without the official wildlife rehabilitation center polo shirt he had been wearing when they had met him.

The two women seemed delighted to see him, and Bob doubted that Debbie was worrying about the license plate number. But why was no one asking what David was doing here, hours away from where they had last seen him?

"It's nice to see you again," Debbie said. She tilted her head toward Bob, like she wanted him to pretend to be equally excited at the unexpected meeting.

"It's certainly a surprise," Bob said, nodding in greeting. Debbie frowned in his direction. He supposed that wasn't what she had in mind.

"It is just as much a surprise for me as it is for you," David said with a chuckle. He sent a glance Sandy's way. "But a good one. I couldn't believe it when Sandy texted me and told me that you are in Carlsbad for a few days."

Sandy blushed and looked away.

"What brings you all the way out here?" Bob asked. "Surely you don't come this far to rescue animals for your rehabilitation center."

"Oh no, not at all," David said. "Didn't Sandy tell you? I only volunteer there a few days a month. My full-time job is actually as a park ranger at the caverns."

Debbie smiled at Sandy. It was the type of smile that women got when they had just heard a piece of juicy gossip. "Now that you mention it, I think she may have said something in passing."

Yeah, right. She just wanted to see how much info she could get out of David. Though Bob had to admit, he was a bit curious himself.

Sandy's blush deepened. "Yes, well, now that the pleasantries are out of the way, shall we head to dinner?" She inched closer to the car, as if it could protect her from any further interrogation.

"Absolutely." David walked around to the driver's side door. "But before we go," he said, looking at Bob, "I wanted to ask if you'd be interested in seeing the bat flight tonight. I'm taking Sandy just a little before sunset, and I thought you two might like to meet us there. Today is my day off, so I could sit with you and answer any questions you have."

"Our own personal guide," Debbie said. "We'd love that."

"Great. See you there," David said with a grin and small wave. Sandy practically dove into the car, as if she couldn't get out of there fast enough.

As soon as they drove off, Bob rounded on Debbie. "What was that?"

She cocked an eyebrow. "What was what?"

"We were on the same page until you saw that the mysterious man was David, and then any reservations you had went out the window. We still don't know the guy."

"How about you put a little faith in humanity and just enjoy a little alone time with me," Debbie said, grabbing his hand and pulling him in. A small kiss was all it took for Bob to relent. Just the thought of being alone with her made his heart rate spike.

"All right, you win," he said with a chuckle and gave her a kiss of his own.

"Besides, he invited us to meet up with them tonight. You'll be able to see that she's just fine."

That was true. If David had less than honorable intentions, he wouldn't have invited them along for part of their date.

The mechanic brought out the keys to the loaner car, and a couple of signatures later, they were on their way to find a place they could stay until Bob's car could be repaired.

"YOU WANT HOW MUCH PER room?" Bob asked, his throat constricting at the thought of all that money.

After visiting every other hotel in town, and finding they were all booked, Bob was desperate. But at this rate, he'd have to spend almost two thousand dollars to rent two rooms for the three nights they needed. And that was assuming the mechanic was correct with his timetable.

"I'm sorry, but at three hundred dollars a night, you are getting a good deal," the hotel clerk said.

"How is that a good deal?"

"With the oil boom, there are more people than accommodations right now," the clerk explained, though he seemed bored by it, like he had already given the same speech several times that day. "When you add in the tourists, and the fact that we are the only hotel that still has availability, we could charge you quite a bit more."

Bob rubbed a hand over his face. He might as well sell his car and buy a new one with the amount of money he'd have to spend to stay in Carlsbad.

"Hey, let's go over here and talk," Debbie said. She nodded toward a couch in the reception area. She seemed to know intuitively that he needed some space to think through the situation. It seemed things kept getting thrown at them, and it was getting harder and harder to escape unscathed.

"What do you think?" he asked, collapsing onto the couch.

"I'd like to know your thoughts first," Debbie said, sitting down next to him.

"Truthfully, I just wanted to spend a nice quiet evening with you," he said, taking her hand in his and rubbing a thumb over her knuckles. "I thought we could drop our stuff off at a hotel, then explore the town together. But instead, we've had to either visit or call a dozen hotels. I'm hungry, and I've just found out that if we don't want to sleep in the car tonight, I have to fork over my life savings."

Debbie rubbed a hand over his back. He could get used to having Debbie by his side, through thick and thin. In sickness or in health.

"What if it was nine hundred dollars and I paid half?" she asked. "And then I bet after we get back home, we can convince Zoe to reimburse the expense, because let's be honest, Amor is oozing money right now."

Bob tilted his head. "How are you going to convince him to cut the price?"

A blush crept across Debbie's cheeks. "Well, that's the thing. I'm not." She leapt from the couch before Bob could question her further. He watched her talk with the clerk, give him her credit card, and then return with a set of key cards. "This one's yours," she said, handing him one. "Don't lose it."

They hauled their luggage onto the elevator and took it up to the second floor. "Which room is yours and Sandy's?" Bob asked.

"202."

"Which one is mine?"

Debbie didn't respond right away, but instead walked quickly down the hallway toward her room.

"How can I go to my room if I don't know which one is mine?" he called after her.

She stopped in front of a room. "It's this one."

"Why couldn't you have just told me that in the first place?" he said with a small shake of his head, though he couldn't help but smile at the peculiar way that Debbie liked to do things. It kept him on his toes. Then he saw the placard next to the door. "This says it's room 202."

"Uh huh."

Bob's stomach somersaulted. "That's how you got it to nine hundred dollars. You only booked one room."

"I knew you'd never agree to it, but it has two queen-sized beds, which is much better than sleeping in a car. Sandy and I will take one of the beds, and you can have the other."

Sleeping in the same room as Debbie. He supposed if they were in the car, they'd be in even closer sleeping quarters than this.

"Just as fair warning, I snore," Bob said. He wanted to get the awkwardness out of the way before she found out at two in the morning.

"And I could sleep through a hurricane," she responded. "If there is an emergency in the middle of the night, you'll probably have to carry me out, because I'm not waking up until seven o'clock."

Bob grinned. "Deal. We make a good team."

She planted a peck on his cheek. "Yes, we do." She unlocked their door and held it open for him. "Shall we unpack before grabbing dinner?"

Bob looked from Debbie to the beds inside. "We can do it later," he said, tossing his suitcase from the doorway. It landed next to one of the beds.

She looked at him incredulously. "Are you afraid to be alone with me?"

"Yes, terrified," Bob answered honestly. He didn't trust himself around Debbie, and there were some boundaries he just wasn't ready to cross. And the only way to ensure they wouldn't be crossed was by staying on this side of the doorframe until Sandy returned that evening.

"How is this different from my salon?" Debbie asked, a teasing glint in her eye as she ran a finger up his arm.

Unwanted chills, and desire, escaped with her touch. Yeah, he definitely couldn't enter that room with her. He certainly hadn't minded it when they'd been alone in her salon, after closing hours. But things were different now, and he didn't want to make any mistakes. Not this time around. Bob couldn't risk losing Debbie again.

"I'll meet you at the car," he said, turning and walking away so fast that he was practically sprinting back down the hallway.

As he waited for Debbie, Bob hit his fist against his forehead in frustration. She seemed ready to start back up where they had left off two years earlier. Why couldn't he? This was what he wanted.

Because Bob knew that with Debbie, if he messed this up, he'd never get a third chance.

Chapter Sixteen

D ebbie stared across the restaurant table at Bob, willing him to return her gaze. But he must have ordered some amazing chicken alfredo, because the plate in front of him had completely absorbed his attention. He'd been acting that way ever since he ran from her at the hotel.

She hadn't intended any ulterior motives when she'd asked him if he wanted to unpack his things—she just hadn't wanted to do it when they were exhausted later that evening. She supposed he could have read too much into things when she threw a little harmless flirting in there. But he was acting so nervous about sharing the same space with her, like she was going to turn into a pouncing lioness or something. She hadn't been that way when they were dating, so she didn't know why he'd think she was now.

Debbie finished off the breaded chicken that was left on her plate, then turned her attention to the small place they had found to eat, since Bob obviously wasn't going to be much of a dinner companion. Even though the restaurant was on the quaint side, it held a certain charm that drew her in. On the other end of the restaurant was a small stage and an area for guests to dance. The stage had been vacant when they first sat down, but a woman with a guitar was now sitting there and tuning her instrument.

A slow and beautiful melody drifted toward them, and it sounded like it was an original composition. Debbie removed the linen napkin from her lap and placed it on the table.

She stood and held her hand out to Bob. He stared at it uncomprehendingly.

"I wasn't quite done yet," he said.

"That doesn't mean you can't take a break," she said, taking his hand and pulling him to his feet.

His gaze met hers. "What did you have in mind?"

"I know you say that you don't dance in public, but we're going to change that—right now." Debbie felt an immediate tug of resistance on her hand.

"Maybe another time."

Debbie tightened her grip and led him to the tiny dance floor, then spun him to face her. "I know you have your anxieties. I do too. But if you can't meet me halfway, then I don't know how this is going to work." Her words seemed to shock him into submission. He was no longer trying to get away.

Bob then surprised her by giving her a lopsided grin. "Dancing with me means that much to you?"

She gave a solemn nod. "It does."

"Then I suppose now is as good a time as any to learn." He placed one hand on her waist and pulled her in as they swayed to the music.

They were quiet, and Debbie liked it that way. Things had been so weird between them, she just wanted his presence right now. This was the first time she'd ever convinced him to dance with her, and she wanted to savor every moment of it.

Just before the song ended, Bob surprised her by sending her into a soft spin and then dipping her in his arms.

She stared up at him. "You know how to dance." There was a slight accusatory tone to her words that she couldn't hide.

Bob helped Debbie to her feet. "A little."

"No, a lot. Like, you *really* know how to dance."

He chuckled and rested his forehead against hers. "I used to. But it's been a long time."

"Thank you." She didn't know how to express what she was grateful for. Maybe that he'd shown that side of him to her. Brick by brick, he was dismantling the barrier he had created for himself and allowing her a glimpse inside.

"People are watching," Bob said suddenly as he glanced around nervously, like the thought hadn't occurred to him before.

"Yes, they are," Debbie said, holding her breath, waiting for him to run away, like always.

"I got caught up in the moment, and nothing but you mattered," he finally said, turning his gaze back to her. "You're the only thing that has ever mattered."

Debbie's breath caught in her throat and she pulled him in. He didn't resist as she kissed him deeply.

There was no going back now.

DEBBIE AND BOB HURRIED into the bat flight amphitheater. Debbie spotted Sandy and David sitting on a rock bench near the front.

"Where have you guys been?" Sandy asked when Debbie and Bob slid in next to her. She and David were looking awfully cozy.

"We had trouble finding a hotel with rooms available," Debbie said. "Then we were starving so we had to get something to eat on the way here." She left out the details about the dancing and kissing session she and Bob had enjoyed at the restaurant. And in the car. And on a darkened path leading up to the amphitheater.

Bob grinned. "Yup. That's what we did."

Okay, he was being completely obvious. What had happened to the stoic Bob who left his emotions hidden? She could use him right about now.

"No worries," David said, returning his grin.

"Did we miss anything?" Debbie asked, turning the conversation.

David gave a quick shake of his head. "Nope, you're right on time. A guide will come out in the next minute to give instructions and talk a little about the bats before they fly out."

The sun was just starting to dip below the horizon, and Debbie took the spare moment to take in their surroundings. Carlsbad wasn't so different from the rest of New Mexico, as it was stuck right in the middle of the desert, but the cavern that gaped in front of them was not so typical. She walked up to a small retaining wall to get a better view. The opening to the cavern was gigantic and looked like it would swallow her if she wasn't careful. A footpath wound its way from where she stood down into the dark hole until she couldn't see where it led anymore.

"You sure you want to go down in there tomorrow?" Bob asked, wrapping his arms around her from behind. His breath tickled her neck.

This was what she had always wanted when they were dating before—for him to be comfortable enough with her that he would show his affection, no matter where they were. And she was loving every minute of it.

"Absolutely." She tried to sound more confident than she felt. The cavern seemed so...ominous.

A man wearing a dark blue shirt with a patch on the right breast pocket and tan pants walked up to them. "If you don't mind having a seat, we will be starting our program now."

Debbie and Bob hurried back to their bench.

"What do you think so far?" David asked, keeping his voice low as the guide up front welcomed the tourists who had gathered that evening.

"This place is amazing," Debbie said. She eyed several small birds that darted around their heads. "I keep thinking those are the bats, though. They sure like the cavern."

"That's because they live there."

Bob leaned in closer, his brows scrunched up, like he was thinking really hard. "They cohabitate with the bats? How does that work?"

David lowered his voice and tossed a glance at the guide, like he was checking to make sure they weren't disrupting the presentation. "The swallows build their nests out of mud and live against the rock right inside the opening. The bats live much further back, and they have opposite schedules, so they don't have much interaction."

"Fascinating," Bob mumbled.

For another twenty minutes, they listened to amazing tales. The guide likened the bat's story to the hero's journey. He talked of the Brazilian free-tailed bats and their travels to Mexico during the winter, and then their long flight back—while pregnant. Debbie gained more respect for the bats when she heard that they had to hang upside down while pregnant, and then had to catch their babies when they were born, so their young didn't fall to the cave floor.

The guide posed the question—who are the heroes? Is it the mothers or the babies, who typically stay with their mothers for only about three weeks?

A little child pointed up to the sky, and Debbie saw a lone bat fly from the mouth of the cavern.

"They are about to emerge," the guide said quietly. "You must remain seated and quiet for the duration of the flight as the bats leave to find their breakfast. They can see as well as we can, despite what you may have heard, but their echolocation helps them find their food and avoid obstacles. Obstacles like us. So please be respectful. Remember, this is their home, not ours." He slipped up the aisle, and a quiet tension settled over the crowd as they waited for further signs that the bats were coming.

A few more bats emerged from the cavern and a young girl screeched in delight. Her mother promptly clamped a hand over the girl's mouth, but she was so excited, her muffled exclamations could still be heard.

What happened next was akin to a flash flood, where you know it's coming, but rather than a small trickle, everything happens at once. A black cloud seemed to appear from nowhere, then quickly formed into a giant funnel in front of the cavern entrance. Another moment later, bats were shooting off into the sky, while others replaced them in the bat tornado. Many bats followed each other into the night, but there were plenty that flew close over the spectators' heads in their hunt for food, and Debbie understood now why they were to remain seated. A few people seemed to be a bit freaked out by it and quickly left, but Debbie thought it was beautiful.

"How many bats are there?" Bob whispered.

David leaned over. "Tonight? Probably only a couple hundred thousand. There will be more as the summer progresses."

Only a couple hundred thousand. That was plenty, in Debbie's book.

They sat in awed silence as they watched the bats. It wasn't long until it was too dark to see the bats clearly, though they were still exiting the cavern.

"Shall we go?" Sandy asked.

They all agreed and kept their heads low as they left the amphitheater.

Bob took Debbie's hand as they walked through the maze of sidewalks that would take them back to the car. "That was incredible," he said. "I know we weren't planning on stopping in Carlsbad, and I wish it was under better circumstances, but I really enjoyed that."

"The awesomeness of the bat flight never gets old, even though I've seen it hundreds of times," David said.

Debbie couldn't help but notice his hand on the small of Sandy's back. It looked like they had gotten to know each other fairly quickly. The worry that Bob had expressed earlier crept up. It wasn't that she didn't trust David, but she knew that Sandy had been sheltered for a long time and would probably be better off if he took things slowly with her.

When they reached the parking lot, Sandy and David hesitated, like they didn't want to part ways.

"I'll see you tomorrow?" Sandy asked, looking hopeful.

"I've already arranged for you three to have a private tour with me first thing in the morning," David said, giving her a small wink. He looked to Debbie and Bob. "I hope you don't mind. I thought you'd probably enjoy a guided tour and took the liberty of signing you up. We'll meet at the visitor center at nine in the morning."

"Mind? Not at all. We'd be delighted," Bob said, clearly over whatever aversion he'd had to David.

"Perfect. Until tomorrow, then."

Debbie and Bob turned to return to the car, but she glanced back over her shoulder and saw David sneak in a kiss. It wasn't anything more than a peck, but it still made her uneasy.

Maybe Bob had been right about needing that background check. Just in case.

Chapter Seventeen

B ob stretched out on the large hotel bed. He usually slept on a
sofa bed, mostly because someone had given it to him and he
didn't want to take the time to go to the big city to mattress shop.
Besides, the sofa bed was ridiculously heavy and he didn't know
how he was going to haul it back out of his apartment, so sleeping
in hotels this past week had been a luxury. Except, this time was
different.

The light from a streetlamp crept through a crack in the
curtains and landed on Debbie as she slept. She'd chosen the side of
the bed that faced his, and he'd been too transfixed to be able to fall
asleep. Her features were so soft, and her expression peaceful. Even
the occasional snore added to the picturesque scene. He could get
used to waking up to that every day.

What-ifs filled his mind. What if they stayed together for
good? Would he get up each morning to make breakfast so that
Debbie wouldn't have to feel rushed before going into the salon?
Would they have a pet? What was he thinking? Of course they
would. Maybe they'd have a whole yard filled with animals. At the
very least, they had to have a rabbit, preferably one that looked like
the rabbit that had brought them together at the animal shelter.

He released a long sigh. These last couple of days had been
amazing. Bob had been able to let go of his fears and inhibitions,
and only focus on Debbie in the here and now. He loved the feeling
of being able to wrap his arms around her whenever he felt like it,

and have her nestle deeper into his embrace. And it wasn't just the physical side of things. He felt like they had connected on a deep level, and that emotional connection had made her more attractive than ever before.

But whenever his vision left the present and his thoughts dwelt on a future with her, the fear came back. He was afraid of losing her. He was scared of all the what-ifs. What if she realized that she deserved so much more than what Bob could offer her? What if all his idiosyncrasies drove her crazy until she couldn't take it anymore?

Debbie shifted in her sleep and mumbled an incoherent thought. Another moment later, her eyes opened halfway. It took a moment before they focused on Bob, and she smiled. "Hi."

"Hi," he said, returning her smile.

She snuggled deeper into her pillow. "What are you doing awake?"

"Thinking."

"About what?"

Bob didn't know how to answer that. Should he tell her that he wanted to marry her and raise animals together and spend every day of the rest of his life making sure she was happy? Or that he was terrified she didn't want the same things as him?

"Us," he said, sticking to the truth, but keeping it simple.

She stared at him, silent but smiling, before she said, "I'm glad there is an 'us.'"

"Me too," Bob said. He wanted to say more, to bare his soul to her. But his fears kept him quiet.

"You should get some sleep," Debbie said, while stifling a yawn. "Who knows what David has planned for us in the morning?"

"Yeah, you too." Bob closed his eyes, as if he would be able to sleep knowing that the woman he loved was only a couple of feet away from him. "Goodnight."

It couldn't have been more than five minutes before he heard Debbie's breathing deepen, and he knew she had fallen back asleep. He opened his eyes, not feeling in the least bit tired, and rolled onto his back.

Bob didn't remember falling asleep, and he wasn't aware of waking up, but a loud noise that sounded like the crashing of cymbals startled him to his feet. His heart racing, he tried to get his bearings, and then realized it was the phone on the nightstand. Bob grabbed the receiver, shocked that it hadn't woken either of the women in the next bed.

"Hello?"

A woman's voice flooded the line, though she sounded more like a machine. "This is the front desk with your seven a.m. wake-up call."

"I didn't order a wake-up call."

"That's my fault," a tired voice said. It had come from Debbie, who was rubbing her eyes while struggling to sit up. "I was afraid we'd sleep in and be late for our tour."

"Oh, I guess we did," Bob told the woman. "Thank you."

He splashed some water on his face in the bathroom to help him wake up fully, then slipped out for some breakfast, giving the women space to get ready. And, if he was being honest, to give himself space as well. It would only be another couple of days before they returned to Amor, and though he was grateful for the extra time, there was one major anxiety that had kept him up after Debbie had gone back to sleep.

Bob still didn't know if he could go public with their relationship. Despite how comfortable he felt with her, he knew that the people they had known for years would be watching, and talking, and making bets on how long they would last—he just didn't know if he could do it.

"OH GOOD, YOU MADE IT. And with one minute to spare," David said, walking across the visitor center's lobby and meeting them by the front doors.

Sandy tilted her head to one side. "Did you think we wouldn't show up?" She had a teasing glint in her eye, though her voice sounded strained, like she was hurt that he'd think such a thing.

"Of course not," he said. He glanced back toward the desk where his co-workers were helping visitors, then sneaked in a quick hug. That seemed to smooth everything over and Sandy was back to all smiles.

"I thought we'd do the basic tour through the caverns, if you're okay with that," David said, switching into tour guide mode. "I didn't know how you'd feel about crawling on your stomachs through tight quarters."

Debbie grabbed Bob's hand, like just the thought of it was giving her an anxiety attack. "Thank you, we appreciate it," she said, squeezing Bob's hand tighter. He didn't mind one bit, and squeezed back to let her know he understood. He wasn't keen about crawling through dark underground corridors either.

"Before we start, however, I need to ask, have any of you visited a different cave with the items you are currently wearing?" David must have sensed their confusion at the question because he said,

"I only ask because bats across the county are at risk of developing white nose syndrome, a disease that can potentially be spread by humans who pick up spores on their shoes or clothes from an infected cave, then visit a new cave where it hadn't been before."

"Does it...kill them?" Sandy asked, her voice small.

"It can," David said. "Fungus invades the part of the bat's skin that isn't covered by fur. We don't think the fungus itself is what hurts them, but it is a nuisance and can disrupt their hibernation patterns. If they try leaving the cave before food is readily available, they starve."

"I haven't been to any caves," Sandy said, holding her hand up like she was going to swear on the Bible.

"Neither have I," Debbie and Bob said at the same time.

"Perfect," David said. "Let's start, then, shall we?"

They walked along the same path they'd used when attending the bat flight the night before, but instead of stopping at the amphitheater, they continued onto the path that would lead them straight into the heart of the beast. Or, at least that was what it felt like. Even during the day, the mouth of the cavern was dark and gaping. The swallows didn't seem to mind, swooping in and out of the entrance as the small group made their way down the winding pavement. As soon as they had gone far enough that the sun was blocked, the air became markedly cooler.

Bob paused to pull a sweatshirt out of the backpack he wore, despite it being a warm day.

"Good idea," Debbie said, pulling out a light jacket.

"Exactly how far are we going down?" Sandy asked. She was holding David's hand, now that he wasn't in his co-workers' line of sight.

David pulled her in closer and gave her a reassuring smile. "About a thousand feet, but we'll take about an hour and a half to wind down there. I won't have you repelling down or anything like that."

Bob whistled. "That's pretty far down. I'm amazed that anyone realized all this was here." There were lights along the path, thank goodness, because all signs of the sunshine that awaited them outside was gone. A sign announced that they had reached the point where if they turned the lights off, the visitors would no longer be able to see their hands in front of their faces.

"They didn't for a long time," David said. "The cavern itself was discovered thousands of years ago, but it only served as shelter. No one ventured deep inside until the early 1900s. It was finally proclaimed to be a national monument in 1923."

Debbie inched closer to Bob. He entwined his fingers with hers.

"Being down here makes you nervous?" he asked.

She shook her head. "I was just imagining what it must have been like for the first people to explore this cavern. They had no nice trail like we do, and no clue to what was beyond the lights they held. There could have been animals, or drop-offs, or..."

"A bottomless pit?" David interjected.

Debbie squeezed Bob's hand again, and he didn't blame her. Just the thought of it made his skin crawl.

"Is there really a bottomless pit down here?" Sandy asked, her voice sounding strangled.

"Yeah, and you'll be able to see it," David said.

Silence fell over the group as they made their way deeper into the cavern. But with the disappearance of the sun came a different natural wonder. Stalactites grew from the ceiling and seemed to come in all sizes and shapes. Some were thin and beautiful, and if Bob didn't know any better, he would have thought they were made out of lace. Others were thick and intimidating.

"Make sure you don't touch anything while we're here," David said. "The oil from your hands can alter the surface where the mineral water flows. It could change the formation of the stalactites, or worse, cause them to break. Not all of them are as strong as they appear."

A few minutes later, Sandy released a yelp. "Oh my gosh, you should really change the lighting on this one."

A formation that looked an awful lot like a monster opening its jaw sat near the path. Stalactites grew inside its 'jaw,' and the way the lighting had been set up, it looked menacing indeed.

David chuckled. "I'll see what I can do about it."

She looked up at him, and Bob could tell that the woman practically idolized the man. The adoration in her gaze was plain, and she seemed ready to follow him to the ends of the earth. "Really?"

"Though you'll have to forgive me if my boss turns me down," David said quickly. "Maintenance in this place is kind of a big deal." He must not have realized how easy it was to get Sandy's hopes up. Of course, how could he? He hadn't known her for long.

The further they travelled down, the more impressive the scene became. After what seemed like hours, they reached an enormous empty room. There were no formations here, only paths that led in different directions.

"There's a place to eat down here?" Debbie said, reading one of the signs. She turned back to Bob with disbelief written across her features.

"Along with a bathroom and a souvenir stand," David said.

"I'll go for the bathroom," Sandy said, raising her hand.

"I'm right there with you," Debbie said, and the two women wandered down the path that would lead them there.

David and Bob stood in awkward silence for a moment.

"Did you want to..." David started, then gestured toward where the men's restroom was.

"No, I'm good," Bob said quickly. Going to the restroom with another man wasn't something he was comfortable with, even a thousand feet underground.

"Yeah, me neither."

After another bout of silence, David said, "There are some benches near the entrance where the women will come out."

"Yeah, okay." Bob hadn't wanted to admit that after an hour and a half of walking, his feet had begun to hurt. He hadn't planned on the caverns being a hike and he hadn't worn the best shoes for the outing.

After what seemed like an eternity to Bob, the women finally came out, oohing and aahing about how beautiful the bathrooms were, and how incredible it was that they could build all that without disrupting the caverns themselves.

"This way," David said, pointing to another path. "You haven't seen the real reason people visit the caverns."

"There's more?" Bob asked, both excited and hoping his feet would hold out.

Debbie released a small squeal and latched onto Bob's arm. "This is so awesome."

They rounded a corner, and found themselves face to face with...an elevator.

"Wait a minute, we just walked an hour and a half. How long would it have taken if we had used the elevator?" Bob asked.

"About sixty seconds. Maybe a few minutes, if there was a line." David grinned, like he had taken them this way on purpose, just to see their reaction.

"I'm glad you didn't tell us about it," Sandy said. "I thought the walk down was beautiful."

It had come as a bit of a shock to realize that, had they chosen to, they could have gone straight to the good stuff. Even as Bob thought it through, he knew that he agreed with Sandy. The beauty of the caverns was in the journey and discovery, and they would have missed so much.

Bob wasn't sure why it pained him to concede to David. Was it because he seemed to be living the life that Bob felt he was meant to have? Volunteering at the wildlife rehabilitation center, being able to spend every day in the caverns—it was the type of peace that Bob wanted for himself.

But then he looked at Debbie and realized that so was she. Hers was the kind of peace that made him excited to get out of bed in the morning and made him want to spend every day of his life being better, overcoming obstacles, and becoming the type of man that she deserved.

And he'd do everything in his power to make sure she never felt the need to walk away again.

Chapter Eighteen

A gasp escaped Debbie as they approached what was aptly named The Big Room. "I bet you could fit a football field in here," she said, though unable to even see where the room ended from where she stood.

"Six football fields, actually," David said.

But it wasn't just the fact that the room was big that made it so spectacular. It was the sheer volume of stalactites and stalagmites that adorned the room, all lit up with lights that made them glow. There were the lacy ones of before, but in greater abundance, like someone had decorated the ceiling for a party. And then there were the ones to their left that looked like...

"It's like a fairy village," Debbie said with delight. Hundreds of small, stout stalagmites grew from the cavern floor, and really did look like a village of little people gathered together for a festivity of some sort.

Her gaze darted from side to side—she couldn't take it all in fast enough. "I'm glad your car broke down," she whispered to Bob, whose arm she had linked her hand through as they walked. Then she realized what she'd said. Bob would have to pay a thousand dollars to fix a car that might not make it another six months, if the rust eating through the bumper was any indication. She threw him what she hoped he realized was an apologetic look. "I only meant because I would have hated to find out that we had driven straight through someplace as amazing as this, without stopping or giving it a second glance."

Bob chuckled and kissed her on top of her head. "I knew what you meant."

It was a small gesture, but that kiss solidified what she'd suspected since they started this journey. She was very much in love with Bob—she had never stopped, despite how much she had tried squashing the emotion—and she wanted to spend the rest of her life with this unlikely, but perfect for her, man.

They wound their way through so many interesting formations that Debbie wished they could stay for hours. She had already taken at least a hundred pictures with her phone, but they didn't capture the majesty of it all. She wanted to somehow imprint it on her brain, ready for recall when she needed a pick-me-up on a hard day.

The further they walked, the darker it became. There weren't as many lights as they made their way around the back of the room, and then, David suddenly stopped.

"We're here," he whispered.

"Where?" Sandy whispered back.

David nodded to their right. "The bottomless pit."

Sandy's eyes widened, and Debbie was sure hers must have too, because just the name made her stomach flip-flop and she instinctively took a step away from the railing.

"There's no reason to fear falling in," he said quickly. "Unless you decide to climb over the railing, which I don't think I have to worry about with you two."

Debbie held tighter onto Bob's arm as she took a tentative step forward and looked at the hole in front of them. It wasn't quite as big as she had expected, but unnerving just the same. She suspected it was wider than it appeared from where they were standing.

"How deep is it?" Debbie asked, her voice quiet, as if anything louder would wake an awful creature that slept within it. Because every bottomless pit needs a creature guarding it. Obviously.

"Bottomless," Sandy said, using air quotes and acting like the answer was clear.

Bob picked up a pebble that had made its way onto the path and tossed it over the railing and into the pit. Debbie held her breath as she listened for the ping, but the rock made no sound. It was like it had disappeared into a vacuum.

Okay, maybe the pit *was* bottomless.

"See?" Sandy said.

"Do you want me to break the mystique of the pit, or keep you thinking that it really is bottomless?" David asked, eying each of them.

"You mean, it's not?" Sandy asked.

"Sorry. It is deep, no question about that. About a hundred and forty feet, to be exact."

Yeah, that was deep. Debbie snuggled further into Bob. He didn't seem to mind and wrapped his arm around her shoulders, bringing her in even closer. "Why didn't we hear the rock hit the bottom, then?" she asked.

"Because the bottom is covered in soft soil and it muffles the sound."

When David said it like that, it seemed so obvious, and silly that Debbie had allowed herself to think otherwise, even for a brief moment. She shook off the heebie-jeebies and decided it was best to approach this part of the tour from a historical perspective, if for no other reason than to not let her mind run away with crazy thoughts again.

"Obviously someone has been able to measure it," she said. "But has anyone actually been down there?"

Just the thought of someone descending into that pit made Debbie's stomach curl again. Maybe they should just move on to something a little less...fear-inducing.

"Sure. I have," David said casually, though he must have known what kind of reaction that would evoke.

Bob stared at him with open-mouthed shock...and was that a bit of envy that Debbie was seeing? "Are you serious?" he finally asked. "You've actually been down there?"

"Yeah, I volunteer for it every year," David said with a small shrug, like it was no big deal. "Unlike you, who test the pit by throwing a pebble to see if you can hear it bounce, most tourists throw garbage, or whatever else they can get their hands on. Once a year, us rangers have to clear out the crap that has been left down there." He paused. "You probably think it's a great adventure, but you wouldn't believe the kind of stuff I've had to clear out from down there." He gave an exaggerated shudder.

"I still think it sounds amazing," Sandy said, her eyes full of reverence for this man that she was clearly falling in love with. Debbie just hoped it was reciprocated and that David wasn't leading Sandy on. "Of course, I'd never do it myself," she quickly amended.

Debbie was impressed by how well Sandy was taking the news that her boyfriend repelled into a deep, dark pit every year. Twelve months earlier, Sandy would have been in full-on panic mode by now, making David promise that he'd never repel into a bottomless hole again.

After another half hour, they found themselves back where they had started the loop around The Big Room, and David graciously suggested they take the elevator back up. It had been a long but awesome three hours, and Debbie was ready for a nap, so she took him up on his offer before anyone else could disagree.

They were just exiting the elevator when Debbie's phone sprang to life. The volume was turned up way louder than she had realized, and she hurried to get it out of her pocket.

Daniel. Oh gosh, no one else could be there for this conversation.

"I just have to take this really quick," she whispered to the rest of the group, and she sped out of the visitor center.

"What do you got for me?" she asked, answering the call and sitting down on a bench overlooking the parking lot. Not the most picturesque view, but she didn't want to wander too far away.

Debbie held the phone between her shoulder and cheek as she searched in her purse for a pen and a pad of paper, just in case she needed to take notes. As she did so, her cheek accidentally pressed the speaker button.

"He's clean," Daniel said, his voice projecting from the phone. "He's cleaner than clean. You should congratulate Sandy on finding such a great guy, because there isn't anyone better."

Relief flooded through her as she slipped the pen and paper back into her purse. "Thanks. I appreciate it."

"No problem. Anything else you need?"

Debbie stood and hoisted her purse over her shoulder. "No, I think that will do it. We'll be back in a couple of days, providing everything goes smoothly with Bob's car."

"I can come rescue you guys if you want," Daniel said.

The offer was tempting, but then they'd have to come back out to get the car. Besides, she was enjoying acting the part of tourist. "Thanks for the offer, but I think Bob would freak out. Without you running the office, who would do it?"

"Good point. See you soon."

"See you."

Debbie ended the call, then turned back to the visitor center to find the others. She didn't have to go far. They were standing in front of the doors, and the moment she saw their faces, she knew they had heard the phone call. "Hey, guys," she said weakly. "Just checking in on things back home."

Sandy's arms were folded across her chest and her eyes narrowed. "Funny that Daniel called you instead of Bob—his boss."

"Yeah, funny." Debbie forced a small laugh. "Should we catch the movie that's playing in the visitor center? It would be interesting to learn more about the caverns."

It only took two strides for Sandy to be standing so close to Debbie that their feet were practically touching. "You had Daniel run a background check on David."

Debbie looked over Sandy's shoulder at David. He gave a small shrug and his gaze dropped. He didn't seem angry, though. "Only because I care about you," Debbie said in a soft voice, her gaze meeting Sandy's. "I like David. I just...had to be sure."

"No, you did it because you don't trust me. No one does," Sandy spat out. "Everyone feels like they have to take care of me, but believe it or not, I don't need it anymore."

"I can see that now," Debbie said, trying to talk Sandy down. Whether it was true or not was a different story. Because it wasn't just about Sandy and whether her judgment could be trusted. It was also about David and being able to trust *him*. If background checks were anything to go by, he was a good guy, but she hadn't known that at the time.

Sandy took a couple of steps back, but her lips were still drawn tight. "I'll get a ride back to the hotel with David." She turned on her heel and walked back into the visitor center without a backward glance.

David looked helplessly between Debbie and where Sandy had disappeared. "If it makes you feel any better, I understand why you did it. You only met me a week ago—I'm practically a stranger. You're a good friend."

"At least someone thinks so."

He gave her a small smile and said, "I'll go talk to her." He gave Debbie a small wave then disappeared into the visitor center.

Bob was the only one left, leaning against the side of the building. A few tourists passed by him before he pushed away and approached Debbie. He pulled her into a hug, and she wrapped her arms around him, clinging on. "I thought I was doing the right thing," she said, fighting a few stray tears.

He smoothed down her hair. "I know you did. I nearly did the same thing myself."

She pulled back, just enough to look him in the eyes, but her arms remained around his waist. "I love you."

Bob's eyes widened for a fraction of a second, then crinkled as a smile exploded across his face. He pulled her back in, crushing her to his chest. "I love you too," he whispered into her ear. "I always have, and I always will."

Nothing else that happened could compare with this moment. Debbie could do anything—conquer anything—because Bob was hers. And that was all she needed.

Chapter Nineteen

Bob placed his suitcase in the back of the loaner car. He glanced at his watch. Debbie had said she'd be right down, but it had already been twenty minutes.

He slipped his sunglasses on and leaned against the car. A couple of years ago, it might have bothered him to wait. But not anymore. Just the knowledge that she still loved him was enough. Bob would wait for another two years, if it meant being with Debbie.

But he didn't have to wait years, or even months. Just a few moments later, she came rushing out of the hotel, suitcase in hand. He stepped forward to help.

"Sorry," Debbie said, allowing him to take her luggage. "I managed to talk the clerk into refunding the extra night that we don't need." She opened the passenger door and leaned against it. "I still don't understand how the garage was able to fix the car so quickly. I thought they weren't going to be able to do it until tomorrow."

"I thought so too," Bob said, slamming the trunk shut. "But the guy said they had ordered the same part for a different car, and somehow both were delivered this morning." He felt like it had been a miracle, and he was grateful for it. It would be nice to be back home, and nicer that he was going back with Debbie.

Bob slipped into the car and fastened his seatbelt, but something felt different—like he had forgotten something.

"Where's Sandy?" he asked abruptly, realizing it wasn't a something, but a someone, that had slipped his mind.

Debbie fastened her own seatbelt, then looked down at her hands, a guilty expression flitting across her face.

"She *is* coming, right?"

Debbie shifted in her seat, still refusing to meet his gaze. After a moment, she shook her head.

Dread settled in Bob's stomach. "Where is she?"

"In the hotel room. Packing."

"So...she'll be right down?" Though he knew this was wishful thinking. Judging from Debbie's reaction, the answer was obvious.

She didn't answer, but instead looked out the window, back toward the hotel, as if that could make Sandy appear. "It's my fault," she finally said. "If I wouldn't have asked Daniel to run that stupid background check..." Her voice trailed off.

The dread began to morph into panic. "What happened?" he asked, trying to keep his voice calm. Freaking out right now wasn't going to help anything. Probably.

Debbie was quiet for a moment before finally speaking. "She wouldn't even look at me last night. Did you notice that she opted to sleep on the hard floor with nothing more than a blanket, rather than share the bed with me?"

Bob nodded slowly. He had noticed, but he'd figured things would be all right by morning. Most things worked themselves out with a good night's sleep. Maybe not this one, though.

"Well, anyway, the silent treatment continued this morning and through lunch until I asked if I could carry her suitcase down for her. She said she wasn't finished, and I said I could wait. That was when she told me she wasn't returning to Amor with us."

Bob couldn't believe Sandy was so angry about it that she wouldn't even sit in the same car with them for a few hours. "How is she going to get back, then? Is there a bus?"

"No," Debbie said, the syllable elongated, like there was bad news on the other end of the word. "She's not coming back at all."

"What?" Bob yelped. He hadn't meant for it to be so loud, but there was no way they could return to Amor without Sandy. First off, how would Sandy fare on her own? She'd never held a job, let alone had a bank account, rented an apartment, or anything else an independent adult needed to know how to do. Second, Rebecca would kill them. Maybe that should actually be moved to the number one spot.

"I know, I know," Debbie said with a groan. "I tried to convince her to come back with us and think through the decision, but she says she has it all worked out. Apparently there are job vacancies at the caverns and David is going to set her up with something—possibly a tour guide, or something in the visitor center."

"But where is she going to live in the meantime?"

"David has that worked out too," she said. "There is an extra guest house on his property that he usually rents out to tourists. She'll stay there until she starts getting paychecks and can find something else."

"So he's just going to give up that extra source of income for a woman he just barely met."

Debbie gave a small shrug. "It looks like it."

Bob groaned and rubbed a hand over his face. "Why are we bothering to return to Amor when Rebecca is going to murder us as soon as we step out of the car? Maybe David can find us jobs at the caverns too."

He was kidding—sort of—but he really didn't know what they were going to do. They couldn't just leave without Sandy.

Debbie reached over and placed a hand on his arm. "We can't hide out here. Sandy told me she'd call her mom to explain the situation. Rebecca will have had time to calm down by the time we get there."

"You're serious?" Bob asked incredulously. "We're going to abandon Sandy."

"No one is *abandoning* anyone," Debbie said, exasperation tinging her words. "This isn't our decision. Whether she acts like it or not, Sandy is an adult and she's found some place where she wants to stay—and, more importantly, someone she wants to stay here with."

Bob knew that Debbie was right, but that didn't mean he needed to like it. "You're sure David's background check came back clean?"

"You heard it yourself. Everyone did. He's a model citizen."

Bob sucked in a long breath before turning the key in the ignition. "All right. I guess we're going home."

THE LAST STRETCH OF the drive always seemed to take the longest, but Bob didn't mind. It had been a relaxed ride as he and Debbie enjoyed the time alone. Even when they hadn't been talking, it was a peaceful silence—one that said they were comfortable with the other person and were just happy to be together. As Bob drove around the final bend, Amor came into view. Debbie gave his hand a squeeze and looked at him, her eyes lighting up.

"It's been a wonderful adventure, but I am so glad to be home."

"Me too," Bob said. He returned her smile, but almost immediately felt the anxiety that had been absent the past few days. He tried shoving it back down. It had no place in his life anymore. Bob had left Amor a miserable bachelor, and he was returning as a new man with an exciting future awaiting him. But there was enough of the old Bob still lurking in the shadows that he couldn't help but worry that he wasn't a completely changed man.

It wasn't until they had pulled up in front of Debbie's home that he was pulled from his own thoughts and he realized she was talking to him.

"I told them we could probably make it," Debbie said. "You don't have anything going on, do you?"

Her words startled Bob, and he could only stare for a moment while trying to wrap his head around what she was saying. "Someone invited us somewhere?" he asked slowly. No one even knew they were dating, so why would someone ask them to come over? As a pair.

Debbie's forehead crinkled, like she was trying to figure out if he was joking. "Yeah. Like I just said, my parents are having a barbecue on Sunday. They only live about forty-five minutes away, so I thought that would be a great opportunity for you guys to get to know each other."

Bob swallowed hard. "Your parents?"

"You're going to have to meet them sooner or later, so why not over some delicious meat?"

He had declared his love for Debbie. He wanted to spend the rest of his life with her. He knew there were certain milestones that had to happen as a result. But meeting her parents? It felt so sudden. "Wait," he said slowly, replaying the conversation. "They invited us over. Like, as a couple."

"Yeah. Is that a problem?" Debbie's gaze had turned intense, like she was warning him to watch what he said next.

"So, you've told them about us." The tug of anxiety Bob had felt was pressing on his chest, making it hard to breathe.

"Last night," Debbie said, completely unaware of what her words were doing to him. "I talk to them a few times a week and I was letting them know that we were getting into town a day earlier than we thought we would."

"Do they have friends here in Amor?" Bob managed to ask. He felt dizzy.

"Sure. I grew up here, remember? They moved after I graduated high school."

Which meant that as soon as her parents told one person, everyone would know. And there would be questions—so many questions. "When did you two start dating?" "Have you set a marriage date?" "How many children do you plan on having?" And then there would be the more intimate and embarrassing questions that the old women in town would ask, not caring that it was completely inappropriate, because, "Hey, we've lived long enough that we get to do what we want now."

Bob had thought he had moved past this. And he had—in Carlsbad. But now that they were back, everything felt different. Why couldn't they have had even a week to themselves and then gradually added in things like walks in the park or dates at the local restaurants? He might have been fine meeting Debbie's parents in a month or two, but this—it was too much, too soon.

"It's a definite possibility. I'll think about it," he finally said, hoping that would buy him some time.

"Is that another way of you brushing me off?" Debbie asked, her brows furrowing. "You used to do this to me all the time. I can't believe we're starting right back where we left off two years ago."

"No, it's not that," Bob said quickly, recognizing the pleading tone in his voice. "I just need a little time—to get used to everything."

Debbie undid her seatbelt with quick motions, and he knew he'd done it again. He'd messed things up. How had it gotten to this point so quickly? She opened her door and jumped out. Bob followed suit.

She yanked her suitcase from the backseat. "I suppose the next thing you are going to say is that, if it isn't too much trouble, you'd appreciate if I asked my parents to not tell anyone we're a couple." Debbie's mouth was set in a firm line, and her eyes seemed to crackle with her fury.

Okay, yes, that had been what Bob was about to say—but not now. He must have hesitated too long, however, because Debbie's mouth dropped open in shock.

"Really?" She stormed up to her front door, but fumbled with getting the right key into the lock.

"Can't we talk about this?" Bob called after her. He hurried across her lawn. "I've changed. Or at least I'm working on it. Let me prove it to you." He was determined not to lose her—not this time. He couldn't bear it.

Debbie finally managed to get the door unlocked and it swung open. "I'm not going to let you break my heart again," she said. "I'm not someone you can hide in a closet until you're ready to pretend we're a real couple with a real relationship."

"That's not my intention," Bob said.

"I believe you," Debbie said, her voice dropping in volume. And she really seemed like she meant it. "But that's not enough. I need someone who will acknowledge that I mean something to them—that I'm something special in their life—beyond closed doors. I have a very close relationship with my parents, and I need someone who is willing to attend family gatherings and town events with me. You can't do that. And I'm not saying it's your fault, or that I blame you. It's just how it is."

"But..." The words died on Bob's lips as he tried to think of something to say. But nothing came out.

"See ya around, Bobby," she said softly before slipping into the house and shutting the door.

"Goodbye, Deb," he said to the empty porch.

He shuffled back down the steps. He knew she was right. It was a repeat of what had happened two years earlier. Except, this time was different. Bob could feel it. There had been a shift on their road trip, and he knew he could change. This wasn't like before.

And he was going to prove it to her.

He jumped into the car and raced down the street, his thoughts speeding just as fast.

Bob was going to win Debbie back.

Chapter Twenty

Debbie walked into the salon and straight back to her office. Her stylists threw a curious glance her way as she passed them, but neither of them said anything. It wasn't like her to come to work sullen and grumpy. She'd be back to her old ways as soon as she nursed this headache. A can of soda and two pain pills should do the trick.

With that out of the way, she eased herself into her office chair and leaned back, propping her feet on the desk. She closed her eyes and wondered what she'd been thinking, coming into work after not sleeping all night. How could she have slept, when Bob infiltrated her dreams every time she tried? Of course, he occupied her thoughts while awake too, so it hadn't seemed to matter either way.

Debbie couldn't get the image out of the head—the one with him standing on her porch, looking at her like she had been the one to kill that rabbit he had spent months raising. He had really believed what he was saying. And she had seen the pain her words had caused him.

But Bob couldn't change, could he? He had been stuck in the same behaviors since he was a teenager—always closing himself off to people. It wasn't his fault, of course. But it wasn't Debbie's either. And she wasn't going to waste years waiting for him to finally admit in public that he and Debbie were in love.

That thought caused her breath to hitch. In love. She was deeply and profoundly in love with Bob. But was that enough to trump everything else?

She didn't come up with an answer, because at that moment, the door to her office burst open, hitting the wall with a bang.

It startled Debbie so badly that she fell out of the chair, toppling it over with her as she landed on the floor beside it. She looked up to see Rebecca glowering down, her hands on her hips.

"I understand that you were missing a passenger on your return trip," Rebecca said.

"It wasn't our fault," Debbie said, scrambling to her feet. "I begged her to come back with us—to think it over."

"Oh, so you talked to her and she said no," Rebecca said with an eye roll.

Debbie held up her hands in a defensive gesture. She reminded herself that Rebecca was just a concerned mother—although more like a terrifying mother bear who had just discovered one of her cubs was missing. "What was I supposed to do?"

"Throw that girl into the back seat with the child locks on," Rebecca retorted.

Debbie lowered her hands. "Sandy is a grown woman. She made her decision."

"She's not ready for that yet."

"I think she is. And it seems like her therapist thought so too."

Rebecca waved a dismissive hand. "Her therapist is a quack."

Debbie cocked her head to one side. "Really? Hasn't Sandy been seeing the same therapist for the last decade and a half?"

"It doesn't matter," Rebecca said, her eyes narrowing. "What matters is that I entrusted my daughter's safety to you, and you lost her along the way."

"Now just one moment," Debbie said, her voice rising. "I know exactly where your daughter is and who she is with."

Rebecca took a threatening step toward Debbie. "Yes, a man she's known for seven days."

"I've spent some time with him and even did a background check. He's a good guy."

"Would you be saying the same thing if Sandy was *your* daughter?" Rebecca was now so close to Debbie that they were nearly touching.

"Like I said, I had no choice," Debbie said. "I was not going to kidnap her."

A figure jumped in between them at that moment and forced them apart. Zoe stood there, facing Rebecca, who was now so angry that her face was nearly purple.

"Let's call this one a tie," Zoe said, seeming slightly out of breath. "I'll talk with Debbie and get all this sorted out, but for right now, I noticed a line forming outside the bakery."

Rebecca threw one more glare at Debbie, then stalked out.

Zoe peeked around the corner of the office, and Debbie heard the tinkling of the bell over the front door.

"Sorry, I got here as soon as I could," Zoe said, setting the office chair upright and sitting in it. She shook her head. "What a mess."

Debbie leaned against the wall, her headache back full throttle. "I did my best, I really did." She paused. "You should have seen Sandy. She was a completely different person while away from her mother. She was relaxed and funny—and confident. There was no way I could have gotten her to come back with me."

Zoe gave Debbie a small smile and nodded. "I'm glad to hear it."

Silence filled the space, and Debbie didn't want to be rude, but it was becoming a little awkward, and she found herself wanting to ask if Zoe needed anything else. It turned out, however, that Debbie didn't need to ask.

"I heard that you and Bob are on better terms these days," Zoe finally said.

Debbie's gaze snapped up to meet the mayor's. "How did you—?"

"Your mother," Zoe said.

"Oh, right," Debbie said with a small chuckle. "Well, you'll just have to start quelling the rumors, because they are no longer true."

Zoe raised an eyebrow. "Over so quickly?"

"Some things just aren't meant to be." It pained Debbie to say it, but what good was it to pretend?

"Well, that's a shame," Zoe said, but the way she said it seemed...odd. Like she didn't believe what she was saying. Before Debbie could question the mayor further, Zoe stood up. "I should get into the office. Just thought I'd save a life before continuing with my other mayoral duties."

Debbie released a wry laugh. "I appreciate it."

Zoe paused in the doorway. "Are you planning on coming by the salsa festival tonight?"

Huh. That was tonight. Debbie really didn't feel like going, especially if rumors about her and Bob were already spreading. It was just going to be another source of pain.

Zoe must have seen Debbie's indecision. "Please say you'll come. Maybe you could even enter the salsa competition."

"I don't cook."

"I didn't mean *that* salsa competition." Zoe grinned. "I hear you are amazing on the dance floor, and there's a man I know who asked if he could be your partner for the competition tonight."

The thought of dancing with another man only served to depress Debbie further. She didn't want anyone but Bob. "I don't think so, but tell him another time. It's sweet that he thought of me."

Zoe's smile drooped and she heaved a long sigh. "He'll be very disappointed. But I have to say, all the women who have been wanting to enter as his partner will be thrilled that you turned him down."

Debbie perked up a little at that. "He's that good of a dancer?"

"And even better looking."

Debbie hadn't danced the salsa with a partner in years. She usually just did it by herself as a way to mix up her exercise routine. It could be fun.

But what if Bob was there? He'd think that in less than twenty-four hours Debbie had managed to move on. Not that it mattered, because they were definitely over. He wouldn't change, and even if he did, she couldn't just wait around for him. She had a life to lead.

Even as she thought it, though, she felt queasy, because she knew it wasn't true. What good was life if you couldn't live it with the person you loved most?

If keeping their relationship secret for right now was the only way she'd be able to be with Bob, she would do it. Time was what he needed, and even if it was years, he was worth the wait.

All of a sudden, Debbie was in the mood for a little salsa. "All right," she said. "I'll do it." She hoped Bob would be there. She needed to set things right.

DEBBIE'S PHONE RANG as she walked to the town park, her blue salsa skirt swishing against her legs. She pulled out her phone, and her finger paused above the green icon. It was Sandy.

"Hello?"

A beat of silence followed on the other end of the line, but Debbie could hear Sandy breathing.

"Are you all right, Sandy?" Debbie asked.

"Yes. Sorry," Sandy said. "I just...I wasn't sure what to say."

Debbie was quiet for a moment, thinking that Sandy would continue. "Are you enjoying Carlsbad?" Debbie finally asked, even though it had only been about a day since she and Bob had left her there.

"Oh yes, it's wonderful," Sandy said, excitement tinging her words. "I'm not quite ready to be a tour guide, but today David introduced me around the visitor center, and just like that, I got a job selling souvenirs right outside The Big Room down at the bottom of the caverns."

"I'm so happy for you," Debbie said, and she really meant it. Sandy deserved good things in her life. Another pause followed. "Well, I guess I better let you go—"

"I'm sorry," Sandy blurted out. "I'm sorry for yelling at you. I know you were just looking out for me."

"Oh, thanks," Debbie said. "But you don't need to apologize. We're all doing the best we can with what we have."

"Just the same, I didn't want to leave things how we did. You've been so nice to me, and I knew you didn't deserve the trouble I caused." Sandy paused. "My mom called me this afternoon...again...and I made sure she knew that none of this is your or Bob's fault. I told her that I had refused to come back with you. I even invited her to come visit in a couple of weeks. I know she'll love David, and then she'll see that everything is just how it should be."

Debbie wasn't sure it would be quite so easy to smooth things over, but she appreciated Sandy's optimism. "The best thing you can do now is to create a happy life for yourself." Debbie turned a corner, and suddenly could hear music coming from the direction of the town park. "I'm sorry, Sandy, but I have to go. Keep me updated on how things are going for you, all right?"

"Sure thing," Sandy said before disconnecting the call.

It seemed that at least one thing had gone in Debbie's favor today. Hopefully, winning the salsa competition would be the second. She entered the park through a small pathway between two stores and was immediately immersed in the excitement that buzzed through the air. Couples strolled on the pathway that snaked around the park and children ran among them, holding tight to colorful balloons. A portable dance floor had been set up on the grass at the far end of the park, and a live band played from the pavilion next to it. She saw that the salsa competition—the edible kind—was already underway, and she made a mental note to volunteer to be a judge next year. She had just wandered over to grab some chips and try a few of the entries when a hand fell on her shoulder.

Zoe stood next to Debbie. She was wearing a tight black top and a flared skirt that was so pink, Debbie was grateful that the sun had already started to set so as to help shield her eyes.

"Hey, you look great," Zoe said, eying Debbie's outfit.

Debbie was suddenly self-conscious and wished she'd gone with a top that covered more skin. there was a gap between her black top and royal blue skirt, and it exposed a lot of her stomach. "Thanks," Debbie said, tugging on the top to try to make it a little longer. She turned back to grab a plate, but Zoe grabbed her arm.

"You can try the salsa later," she said, pulling Debbie away from the food. "You need to register and get your number for the dance competition."

Debbie cast a longing gaze at the fresh salsa, but followed Zoe toward the dance floor. "So, where's my partner?" Debbie asked. "I was hoping to run through a couple of routines with him beforehand."

Zoe stopped in front of a table, where she grabbed a large white square with the number twelve on it. "Just put your name next to the twelve on this sheet, and you'll be good to go."

Debbie did as instructed and felt Zoe pinning the number to the back of her top. "Do you know what time he'll be getting here?"

"Who?" Zoe asked, sounding distracted.

"My partner. The one I'm supposed to be competing with? It's going to be a little difficult if I've never danced with him before."

"Oh, right. Him. He'll be here." Zoe sounded like it wasn't a big deal, and almost like she'd forgotten that Debbie had a partner in the first place.

"When does the competition start?"

Zoe stepped around Debbie. "Fifteen minutes."

Debbie looked around and noticed other dancers filtering in onto the dance floor and start warming up. With their partners. She had a sinking feeling that hers was going to be a no-show. And she was going to be left looking like an idiot—all dressed up with no one to dance with. "Maybe this wasn't the best idea," she said, taking a step backward. "I can run home and change and be back before much has happened."

Zoe spun back toward Debbie, a hint of panic in her eyes. She grabbed Debbie's arm and steered her toward the dance floor. "Don't be silly. This is exactly what you need."

Debbie really didn't think so, and said as much, but Zoe didn't seem to hear her.

"Just warm up with a few stretches and dance routines that you enjoy, and those pre-competition jitters will slip away," Zoe said with a wide smile, though her eyes darted everywhere else and couldn't seem to settle on Debbie.

"O-kay," Debbie said. She practiced the moves that she often did with her exercise routine and started feeling better about it. Worst case scenario, even if her dream partner didn't show up, she could still show off some awesome moves. Debbie had to force herself to keep looking at the positive side of things, because really, she wanted to be anywhere but there. Why had she let Zoe talk her into this? She just wanted to be home.

Someone with a microphone announced that the salsa dance competition was about to begin and asked the participants to take their places on the dance floor. There was only one rule. Any contestant whose shoulder was tapped was out of the competition.

Debbie's gaze finally found the person the voice belonged to.

Rebecca.

Was she one of the judges? Debbie hoped that Rebecca was only in charge of the announcements, because with the glare that she sent Debbie's way just then, Debbie would be the first one to leave the competition.

It looked like Debbie's partner was a no-show, but she held her head high and found a place among the couples on the dance floor.

The music started and Debbie felt the music flow through her. Her hips and feet knew what to do and she found it easy to lose herself in the music, allowing the stresses of the previous day to melt into the dance floor.

Debbie spun in place, but was stopped short when she ran into someone. "I'm so sorry," she said, her hand landing on a man's chest. He wore black pants and a loose blue shirt that had a V neck so low, she could almost see his belly button. She took a step back, but he grabbed her hand.

Her gaze met his, and she couldn't contain the small gasp that escaped her lips.

"I believe we're partners for this dance," Bob said, the corner of his lips slightly upturned. He spun her, then brought her into him.

Debbie slipped her hand from his, then pinched herself. "Is this really happening?" She looked him up and down. "There is no way the real Bob would ever wear something like that."

"Not even if he loved competitive ballroom dancing when he was in high school?" Bob held out his hand to Debbie once more.

She shook her head and laughed. "All right, let's see what kind of moves you have."

And boy, did that man have moves. From the second her hand touched his, they were unstoppable. There was an energy about Bob that transformed the way she danced, and no matter how many spins and dips they did, nothing could slow them down.

Bob had her fixed in an intense gaze the entire time, and it seemed that the other competitors had disappeared and it was just her and Bob, in their own sphere, dancing to the music they had created for themselves.

It wasn't until Debbie heard applause that she slowed enough to take in their surroundings.

They were the only ones left on the dance floor, and it appeared that the applause was for them. Debbie spotted Daniel and his wife Melinda on the edge of the dance floor, clapping. Zoe stood next to them with her husband, Stephen. But they weren't the only ones. Everyone else was on their feet as well, clapping and hollering. Well, everyone but Rebecca.

"Did we just win?" Debbie asked, her breath coming out in gasps.

Bob still held her hand, and he lifted it into the air above their heads with a cheesy grin on his face. "Why yes, I think we did."

They were ushered up to the front of the stage, where there was a small platform. Debbie's fingers curled around Bob's as they stepped onto it. Rebecca stood in front of them, and though she didn't look like she was enjoying it, she placed a medal first around Debbie's neck, then around Bob's.

Rebecca was just walking away when Bob grabbed Debbie around the waist and planted a long, firm kiss on her lips.

An explosion of gasps mingled with catcalls erupted from the crowd. Debbie's face burned with both pleasure and embarrassment. When Bob pulled away, she looked him in the eyes.

"You just kissed me. In front of every person we know."

He grinned. "Yes. I did. And you know what else I'm going to do in front of every person we know?"

Debbie's head swam as Bob dropped to one knee in front of her, then reached inside his shirt and pulled out a box. She was giddy and nervous and astounded and confused.

But as he asked her to marry him, one emotion rose above the rest.

Delirious happiness.

"Yes!" she screamed, tackling him so they both fell to the ground. The crowd laughed as she and Bob attempted to disentangle themselves long enough for him to get the ring on her finger.

"Yes," she whispered again, placing her hands on the sides of his face. "It's always been yes."

The End

About the Author

Kat Bellemore is the author of the Borrowing Amor clean romance series. Deciding to have New Mexico as the setting for the series was an easy choice, considering its amazing sunsets, blue skies and tasty green chili. That, and she currently lives there with her husband and two cute kids. They hope to one day add a dog to the family, but for now, the native animals of the desert will have to do. Though, Kat wouldn't mind ridding the world of scorpions and centipedes. They're just mean.

You can visit Kat at www.kat-bellemore.com.